HER WAGON TRAIN COWBOY

LONDON JAMES

ONE

LILLIAN

A knock rapped on the front door. Lillian looked upon the chunk of wood, and her heart thumped. She wished her husband was here to answer it. He always knew what to do and say to whoever came by the house. Sometimes it was beggars. She never did like this part of town, but it was the one place they could afford on his wages at the sawmill, and although her parents often offered Lillian and Jacob a place to stay in their house, Jacob never wanted to take them up on it. It wasn't that he didn't love his in-laws; he just always felt guilty for her parents buying stuff for them because he made so little money.

Whomever it was knocked again, using a bit more force behind the movement, and the pounding rattled the wall, shaking the shelf next to the door. The books sitting on the shelf flopped over, and Lillian flinched.

She inched over to the door, steadying her breath as she glanced at the window. She could look out and see who it was. Perhaps she could even do it without them noticing or seeing her. Or she could ask whom it was, deciding only after they answered if she wanted to open it or not. She had been getting more visitors lately since her husband's death. People wanted to extend their deepest sympathies by bringing *her different baked goods or bushels of fresh vegetables. She had welcomed the food as she had little money and rent was due if she decided to stay in this house without Jacob instead of move home to her parents.*

The person knocked again. This time the force knocked a couple of the books off the shelf.

"Mrs. Miller, we know you are in there," a male's voice said.

We?

There was more than one?

"Please open the door. We only wish to speak to you. Nothing more."

She sucked in a deep breath and reached for the doorknob, not knowing if she would come to regret twisting it or not.

Two gentlemen stood on the porch, and they both smiled and removed their hats as she greeted them. "What can I help you with today, Gentlemen?" she asked.

"We've come to see about discussing a matter with you, Mrs. Miller. It's about your husband. May we come in?"

"Are you with the sawmill?" While she didn't recognize the two men standing before her, she also couldn't say with certainty that she knew everyone who worked at the sawmill or lumber yard. There were far too many workers, and she'd only met a handful of them.

"May we come in?" the taller man asked again. He was dressed in a nice suit and had a little tuft of banded flowers in his lapel.

Her stomach twisted, but she nodded and opened the door a little wider, letting the two men inside. The shorter of the two hadn't spoken but was dressed just as nice, and he placed his hat back on his head as he followed the taller man inside and stood next to the table with his hands clasped behind his back. His eyes never left the taller man.

"I'm afraid I have nothing to offer you if you are hungry," she said.

"It's quite all right. We want for nothing."

"So, you didn't say, are you with the sawmill?" She brushed her hand across her face as she remained by the door. It would be her only escape should she have the need.

"No, we are not."

"But you said you were here about my husband. Why else would you be here if you didn't work for the sawmill?"

"Mrs. Miller, are you aware that your husband borrowed money from Mr. Sanderson?"

Her gut twisted a little at the man's words. "No. Jacob never mentioned borrowing any money. Are you sure he did?"

"Yes, I'm quite sure."

"Well, I knew nothing about it and still don't know anything. I never saw any money. He never came home with anything other than his wages."

"And you are sure about that?" The taller man ducked his chin, glancing at the shorter man who unclasped his hands and then folded his arms across his chest. He inhaled a breath, and his hardened stare made Lillian's stomach twist even more. She couldn't deny that although she didn't know much about Mr. Sanderson, she did know that he had a reputation in town.

And it wasn't a good one.

Why would Jacob borrow money from such a man?

"Of course, I'm sure. Jacob was a good man. He . . . yes, we didn't have much, but we had enough. We didn't have the need for a loan. Not for anything."

She bit her lip at her lie. Well, half-lie. She was truthful in that they had enough, or at least she had thought they did. But she also remembered a conversation about three weeks before Jacob died that he wanted more for them. He just didn't know how to get it.

Surely, he didn't go seek out Mr. Sanderson for a loan.

Did he?

A lump formed in her throat, and although she tried to swallow it, she couldn't.

"So, what are you here for today, Gentlemen?"

The taller man gave a slight snorted laugh and ducked his chin, glancing sideways again as though to make eye contact with the shorter man behind him. He clasped his hands at his waist.

"Isn't it obvious, Mrs. Miller?"

"No. I'm sorry, but it's not. I don't know anything about any money, so I can't be of any help to you."

"But the debt is still yours."

Her breaths shortened and quickened. "I don't see how it is when I know nothing about it."

"But you can't prove that you don't know other than just saying you don't."

"And what does it mean?"

"It means you still owe the debt."

She gripped the doorknob, and as her palms started to sweat, they slipped on the brass. "I don't have any money."

The taller man stepped forward. His stance towered over hers, and he inhaled and exhaled a deep breath as he looked down upon her. There was nothing but harsh darkness behind his gaze, and he clenched his jaw. "I'm afraid Mr. Sanderson isn't going to take that news well."

"I'm sorry, but I don't know what else to say or do. I'm nothing but a poor widow. And I knew nothing of the money."

"I'm afraid that doesn't matter. Dead or not, your husband owes the money, and because he is gone, that debt is passed to you. You have one week."

"One week to what?"

"One week to get me five hundred dollars."

She sucked in a breath. What would Jacob need or want with five hundred dollars?

"And what happens if I don't have it?"

"I don't know if you want to know the answer to that." Although he didn't say what would happen, his tone and how he furrowed his brow told Lillian she didn't want to know the answer either. Or if she did, she wouldn't like it. Torture, death, every possible haunting way someone could get revenge on a person crossed her mind. He moved past her, heading for the door after motioning the shorter man to follow him. He paused before leaving and looked at her. "And don't *think about going to your parents. If you don't have the money, we have no problem getting it out of them."*

The men walked out, slamming the door behind them.

And Lillian's eyes opened.

*S*omeone had said once that we live out our fears in our dreams. Lillian didn't know if it was true, but having the same one over and over again since the day those men came to her house to visit her, she had lived through the same terrible moment.

Over and over again.

They haunted her every night, and in each dream, she'd awake when they slammed the door. It was the part of her life that she dreaded the most, and at times, she almost didn't want to go to sleep at all.

She rolled over, staring at the horizon. Although it was morning, the sun had yet to peek over the hills of Nebraska or light up the sky with brilliant colors of pink, yellow, orange, blue, or even purple. She sat up, glancing around the camp. Although a few of the campfires still burned, everyone was asleep. Still dreaming their own dreams peacefully in the stillness of the early dawn. She envied all of them.

Well, mostly.

It wasn't proper to feel too much envy for someone. Or she supposed even just a little.

She slid out from under the blankets, checking on her parents, who were sleeping in the back of the wagon, before grabbing her wrap and a bucket. With no chance of falling back to sleep, there was no sense in lying there when she could get a few chores done even if she didn't feel good.

Which was normal.

Or at least normal for her lately.

She didn't want to think about why she hadn't felt good the

last several weeks since leaving home. Thinking about it would only make her more aware that her body wasn't hers anymore. At least not entirely. But instead, she shared it with another who was half of her and half of Jacob.

It was the parting gift of her dead husband.

And it was the only link to him she had left.

The tall blades of grass swished from side to side as she made her way down to the river. Early morning birds flew from the safety of the tall grass while rabbits hopped in different directions, their sudden movements caused her to flinch, and she covered her mouth a few times to keep from screaming. She didn't want to wake anyone—or worse, scare them—at the camp, and with a glance over her shoulder, she continued down the riverbank to the water. She knelt in the sand, not caring about the fine grains digging into her knees through her dress. Frogs croaked along the river, and the crickets chirped. The air around the water felt cooler, and she closed her eyes and inhaled a deep breath.

Unfortunately, it wasn't just the smell of the sweet grass that tickled her nose.

A pungent scent of cattle manure left by the cattle on the other side of the river hit her nose like a wagon barreling out of control down a hill. Her stomach twisted, her mouth watered, and it was only a few seconds later that she retched in the sand.

Her eyes watered, and her throat burned, and when she was finished, she scooped up some of the water in her hands, swishing it around her mouth, before spitting it back out and cupping her hands below the water to get another mouthful.

"You shouldn't do that," a voice said behind her.

She jumped and spun in the sand, meeting her mother's gaze as her mother, Margaret, made her way down to the river and stopped next to her. Margaret looked down at her daughter and smiled.

"Did I wake you?" Lillian asked, looking up at her mother.

Margaret shook her head. "No. I woke up on my own. When I noticed you and a bucket were gone, I figured you'd come down here."

"I just thought I would get started on breakfast, so it was ready for you two when you woke up." Lillian scooped the water again and took it to her lips.

"Don't do that." Her mother slapped at her hands.

"What are you doing?"

"That water isn't boiled."

"Oh." Lillian shook her hands and wiped them on her dress. "Oh, how foolish of me."

"Mr. Russell said Cholera isn't as prevalent around these parts, but you never know. It's best not to drink it until it's been boiled."

"Of course. I . . . I should have remembered. I was just trying to get this taste out of my mouth."

"Did you get sick again?" Her mother knelt in the sand beside Lillian and laid her hand on Lillian's shoulder.

"Yes. I did."

"I've meant to talk to you about how you've felt since we left home."

"I think it's just the stress of it all and riding in the wagon. The motion just turns my stomach."

"Is that all it is?"

"Do you not think it is?" Lillian turned to look into her mother's eyes. So full of concern, the sight of them almost made Lillian tear up.

"No. I don't. And I haven't for a while." Margaret laid her hand on her daughter's shoulder. "But there is nothing we can do or say about it now. I think a new start in Oregon will be what you and this child need."

Lillian snorted. "A new start? And what will that look like?"

"I don't understand."

"What respectable man will want a woman with a child?"

"You are a widow, Lillian. There is no shame in that or in that baby in your belly. Nothing is standing in the way of finding a proper man for you to marry."

Lillian wanted to argue, but she knew it was best not to. Not because she feared what her mother would say or think but because she didn't want her mother to be upset. Lillian saw it differently, no matter what her mother thought of the situation. Sure, she was married when she conceived the child, but she wasn't a wife anymore, and for a man to take on the responsibility . . . well, she just didn't know if a man would want to, much less choose to.

And the thought of a new life in Oregon suddenly felt like a weight on her shoulders she didn't know if she could carry.

TWO

EVERETT

*E*verett blew out a breath as the sky began to lighten around him. His eyes fluttered, and his head bobbed. It had been a long night watching the cattle. He was tired, and his body ached from sitting in the saddle all night. All he wanted was his bed, and yet, he knew as sure as the sun would rise, getting any rest in the daylight hours when the whole camp was alive would be difficult. He was never one to sleep during the day, even if there were times he wished he was different. It was a quality he hadn't inherited from his father.

Although he was actually grateful for that.

And for all the other things he didn't inherit from the man.

He glanced down at the saddle horn, trying not to let himself think about his father or his mother. They'd made their decisions, and while he'd never tell Emma this, he was almost glad he'd never see them again. He never wanted to be reminded of their mistakes or what they'd done to their children—mostly Emma. Ruining her chance at a life lived with Edward Longfellow.

Of course, he couldn't deny it'd turned out better for her. She was happy with James, and Everett was happy for her. She'd found a richer, deeper love, and the excitement for a life lived with the man she was meant for just enveloped every thought in her mind and movement of her being.

He almost envied her.

Even if he thought it would be different for her.

And for him, if he was honest with himself.

He always thought he'd take over the family business, stay in Boston, marry some daughter of one of their friends—keeping it in the high society social circle; his mother would always say —and live out the rest of his years just as he'd lived the first twenty-two of them.

Sure, there were times he didn't like that life with the parties, the suits, the meetings—all mindless duties that drove him crazy from time to time. However, he hadn't known anything different. It was . . . well . . . normal.

Not like it is out here, he thought to himself. *It's not like it is out here at all.*

He inhaled a deep breath, fighting a yawn as he glanced over the cattle grazing on the tall prairie grass. Muffled voices trailed over the hill from the river, and he narrowed his gaze as though the act of it would help him not only see better but hear better. It didn't work, and he cued his horse to turn and trot toward the river while lowering his hand to the butt of the rifle just in case. His heart thumped at the thought of coming across more bandits.

He'd already seen enough of those men. He didn't want any more trouble.

Not now.

Not ever.

"Hello, Mr. Ford," Mrs. Jones waved at him as she crouched next to her daughter, Lillian, then stood. A smile spread across her face, and she cocked her head to the side.

"Mrs. Jones, it's you. I'm sorry for the interruption. I just heard voices and thought I would check out who it was." The tightness in his shoulders relaxed, and he rested his arms on the saddle horn. His horse danced for a second, then seemed to calm too, as it chewed on the bit and lowered its head.

"My daughter and I were just getting some water for the camp."

"It's a bit early for breakfast, isn't it? I mean, we aren't heading out this morning, are we? Mr. Russell said we were staying at least one more day, the last I heard."

"No, we aren't heading out. Neither of us could sleep, so we thought a nice warm breakfast would help." She glanced at her daughter, who ducked her chin and remained kneeling in the sand near the river's edge and staring at the water. She sniffed and wiped her cheeks as though she was wiping away tears.

He hadn't seen much of her since the bandits took her and the men—himself included—rescued her. Surely, it was a harrowing experience for her. He saw how it affected Emma and the nightmares she had had because of it. He also saw, however, how much James had helped Emma through her pain, and knowing Lillian didn't have someone like that, he could only imagine it was that much harder.

A hint of guilt twisted in his stomach. He hadn't checked on her or asked how she was doing since everything happened. While he didn't know her well, she was Emma's friend, and he should have cared more about how she was doing and feeling.

"I think a warm breakfast sounds just about nothing short of heaven. I hope you enjoy it."

"Would you care to join us? I imagine you're hungry after a long night of watching the cattle."

For a moment, he considered saying yes. Not only did food sound good right about now—and his stomach even growled with the mention of it—but he thought it would be a good chance to see how Lillian was fairing after the ordeal. But there was also a slight hesitation in him. Perhaps saying yes would be overstepping somehow.

"Oh, you don't have to do that, Mrs. Jones."

"It's not a bother, Mr. Ford. In fact, Mr. Jones and I would love to have your company as well as Lillian after what you did for her. It would be our pleasure." Mrs. Jones brushed her hand against her chest as she looked toward her daughter, who was still kneeling in the sand and staring at the water.

Everett opened his mouth to say no, but closed it and smiled, giving her a nod. "Well, all right, then. I will accept your kind invitation. I just need to make sure James is awake so he can take over the shift watching the cattle."

"Sounds good. It will be a while before breakfast is ready. But I will send Lillian to come for you when it is." She reached for her daughter, touching Lillian's shoulder. At her mother's touch, Lillian stood and glanced at Everett as she turned to leave the river. Although she smiled, there was pain behind her eyes, which turned in his stomach. He didn't know why, but he didn't like seeing that look in the girl.

He didn't like it at all.

~

*E*verett rode back to the wagons and climbed down out of the saddle. As he tied the horses' reins on the back of the wagon, James sat up from his bed on the other side and wiped his eyes.

"Is it time?" he asked.

"Just about." Everett continued making the knot and grabbed the bucket of water, offering it to his horse, who drank several gulps.

"Did anything happen?" James yawned and rubbed his face before slipping his boots on and standing.

"Not a thing. The cattle stayed where they should, and it was just one boring night."

"I don't know whether or not that's a good thing." James

chuckled. "It's good that nothing happened, but boring nights make for long nights."

"You can say that again." Everett rubbed his own eyes and took off his hat, running his fingers through his hair before putting the hat back on.

"I take it you're going to try to get some sleep now?"

"I will go in a bit. I was invited to have breakfast with Mr. and Mrs. Jones . . . and Miss Jones."

James raised one eyebrow. "Invited? When?"

"Just a bit ago. Mrs. and Miss Jones were down by the river. They asked. I told them I would."

"What were they doing down by the river before the sun is even up?"

"I don't know. Miss Jones seemed upset about something. I can't imagine how it's been for her. I mean, I've seen how Emma's been. I don't know why I didn't think Miss Jones would have the same feelings."

"Yeah, I can't imagine she doesn't either."

"Truthfully, I feel kind of guilty about it."

James bent down, grabbing his blankets and folding them. "Guilty? About what?"

Everett shrugged. "Not checking on her."

"I didn't know you and she were that close."

"You don't have to be close to someone to check on them to make sure they are all right." Everett had a slight growl to his voice, and he furrowed his eyebrows. It wasn't just the tone James used but the words and the hint behind them. It was almost as though he accused Everett of feeling something when he didn't.

"I never said you did." James raised his eyebrow again and stretched before moving over to the campfire and bent down, grabbing a chunk of wood in one hand and a stick in the other. He poked around the fire, setting the new wood on the flames to reignite them. "You seem rather defensive of it, though."

"I don't mean to. Perhaps I'm just tired."

"Perhaps." James shrugged and finished tending to the fire before he moved to the wagon and fetched the supplies to make coffee and some breakfast of his own.

"Of course, it also could be because I feel as though you are implying something."

"What could I possibly be implying?" James paused with his hands full of a pan, wrapped bacon, several potatoes, and the kettle for the coffee.

"I don't know." Everett shrugged with his lie. He did know. He just didn't know if he wanted to say it. "I guess you sound like you're implying I like the young lady or have feelings for her outside of her being a friend of Emma's."

"Well?"

"Well, what?"

"Well, is it possible you do?"

Everett shook his head. "That's absurd. I've barely talked to the woman. I know her name and that she's traveling with her parents, and that's it. How could I possibly like her as anything more than just another lady on this wagon train?"

"I don't know. Because you hugged her after rescuing her?" James threw his hands up in the air.

"She was crying. I only meant to comfort her."

"Well, what about the fact that she's pretty? I mean, she's not as pretty as Emma is to me. But I know you're not attracted to your sister . . ." The two men made the same disgusted face before James continued. "So, I just thought maybe you might have noticed her."

"Well, I did notice her." Everett waved one arm as he turned away from James for a moment. He inhaled a deep breath. This conversation was not going how he expected it to nor wanted it to, and it needed to end. "But noticing someone and liking them enough to court them or marry them---"

"Whoa. Who said anything about you marrying the girl?"

"No one. I . . . that's not what I meant. I . . . I don't think about Miss Jones in that way."

"All right. I'll take your word for it."

Everett waved his hand. "I should head over to their wagon. See if breakfast is ready." He took several steps before stopping and turning back to James with his finger pointed at the soldier. "Don't you dare say a word to Emma."

James held up his hands. "Oh, don't worry. I won't. I'm not about to get in the middle of you two."

THREE

LILLIAN

*L*illian wiped the sweat from her brow as she knelt by the campfire and prodded the wood and kindling. The flames reignited and burned high in the air for a moment before settling back down to the perfect heat and temperature for the pans. She set the kettle on the fire first, starting with the coffee, while her mother gathered the supplies from the wagon and set them down in front of her.

"Do you want to cut up the potatoes or shall I?" her mother asked.

"I will." She held out her hands, taking the potatoes from her mother before setting them on the wood slab they used to cut and prepare the food. One of them rolled off and landed in the grass, and Lillian grabbed it, blowing on it and rubbing it with her hands before setting it back down with the rest.

"Are you feeling better?" her mother asked.

"A little. It only lasts for a little while in the morning; then it goes away."

"I've noticed. I must admit, at first, I thought it was just the trail and the wagon. I know I've gotten sick to my stomach a few times riding in that bouncy thing."

The two women laughed.

"I thought it was, too," Lillian said. "Although, I kind of knew it wasn't."

"Did you know when we left home?"

"No. Jacob and I spoke of starting a family, but then he . . ."

"He died."

Although her mother finished her sentence, the words were no less easy to hear than they would have been to say. Lillian had long since made a choice not to live mourning her husband forever. He was gone. There was nothing she could do but continue to live her life and move on. It would have been what he wanted. But the choice was still hard to make and one she questioned from time to time.

"Have you thought of any names?" Her mother smiled and handed her an onion to chop. Lillian's stomach twisted with the smell, but she took the white root vegetable and set it down with the potatoes.

"No. Not yet."

"Well, there is time. Perhaps Jacob Jr. if it is a boy. Although, I don't know if that would only make it harder."

"I don't think it would. Perhaps I will go with that. It seems fitting, and I would like to bestow that honor."

Her mother smiled again and inhaled and exhaled a deep breath. "Mr. Ford sure seems like a nice man."

"Yes, I suppose he is."

"Have you spoken to him much?"

Lillian shook her head.

"Has Emma said anything about him?"

"Like what?"

"Oh, I don't know." Mother shrugged, and her lips shifted to the side of her face oddly as though she wanted to convey a sense of unknown to her thoughts. Or perhaps it was that she wanted to appear as though she wasn't prodding her daughter with questions even though Lillian knew she was. "Like . . . for instance, if he's traveling to Oregon with the intentions of marrying a woman there or if he has intentions of marrying at all."

"Mother, please, don't."

"Don't what?"

"You know, don't what. Don't ask those kinds of questions."

Her mother rested her hands on her hips and then knelt, holding her hand as though she wanted Lillian to give her a potato. "I don't know what you're talking about. I was just asking normal questions that any mother would ask a daughter about her daughter's friend's brother."

Lillian cocked her head to the side. "Do you even hear how foolish that sounds?"

"Oh hush, young lady." Mother waved her hand and took a potato, holding it while she swiped at the side with the blade of a knife, slicing the skin off.

"I'm sorry, Mother. I shouldn't have said what I did."

"Oh, I know you were just mocking me." Her mother glanced at her, looked away, then looked back. "Right?"

"I suppose I was—a little. But I don't talk to Emma about her brother because there is nothing to talk about. Perhaps if it was just me . . . but it's not."

"What if you talked to her about it? Asked her if he would care."

"I'm not going to do that. None of the women know I was married, and none of them know about the baby."

"Why haven't you told them?"

Lillian shrugged. "I don't know. I just didn't. And now it would seem so odd to tell them after all these months of knowing them."

"But they are your friends. You should tell them."

Lillian sucked in a breath and held it a bit before blowing it out. She knew her mother was right, and she should tell her friends the truth. She didn't know why she hadn't told them. It wasn't that she felt ashamed. She had been married to Jacob. They hadn't lived in sin.

Well, at least she thought they hadn't.

She glanced at her mother, knowing the omission that sat on the tip of her tongue.

It was about the loan he'd taken out with Mr. Sanderson and the one detail she hadn't told anyone. Not even her parents. After the men left her home that day, she packed up all her belongings and headed to her parents. She didn't tell them why, only that she wanted to leave, needed to leave, and start a new life somewhere else. Somewhere far away. And she needed to leave immediately. She knew if she begged, they would help her, and help her, they did. They packed up their whole lives, sold everything, and agreed to come with her to Oregon.

No questions asked.

They were packed and had left two days before the men were supposed to return to her house. She never found out what Jacob had borrowed the money for, nor did she know what had happened to it.

Her mother looked at her, watching her peel the potato before cutting it into chunks and tossing it into the pan. She inhaled and exhaled a breath.

"I suppose if you don't wish to talk to them, you don't have to. Of course, it's your choice."

"I know, and I know I should. I'm just not sure I'm ready."

Her mother laid her hand on her shoulder. "I understand. I won't bring it up again."

"And what about Mr. Ford?" Lillian glanced over at her mother as her mother smiled.

"Oh, well, on that . . ." Her mother bit her lip. "On that, I'm afraid I can't make such a promise."

Her mother laughed, and as she opened her mouth to argue, she caught sight of Everett Ford walking up to the wagon. He lifted his hat, nodding toward them.

"I hope I'm not too early," he said.

"Not at all." Mother stood and pointed toward the log they sat on near the fire. "Have a seat. I'll make you a cup of coffee."

EVERETT

*E*verett sat on the log while Mrs. Jones poured him a cup of coffee. She handed him the steaming cup, and he felt the warmth of the liquid on the palms of his hands. The early morning air was far from cold, but there was a crispness to it that made the cup feel nice in his hands.

"Thank you," he said.

"You're welcome." She poured another cup and sat down on the other log.

"Is that for Mr. Jones?" Everett asked. "Is he awake?"

"Oh, no. Well, I think he's about to wake. In fact, I should go and see where he is. But, no, this is for me." She took a sip, watching Everett watch her as the cup went to her lips and back down into her lap. "Are you all right, Mr. Ford?"

"Everett, please, ma'am, and of course. I'm perfectly all right."

"You haven't seen a woman drink coffee, have you?"

"No, ma'am."

She cocked her head to the side. "And what do you make of it?"

"I beg your pardon?" He cleared his throat, glancing at Miss Jones, who had her head ducked toward her chin while she chopped potatoes and onion.

"I'm just curious as to what you think about women who . . . might not fit the image of a proper woman, or at least has lived outside the lines. One who pushes against the boundaries or might not have the normal past that other young women have." Mrs. Jones cocked her head to the side as she spoke, and as she finished her sentence, she drew out the time between her words as though she wasn't even trying to hint at what she was asking.

"What is normal to you, Mrs. Jones?"

"Oh, I don't know."

He got the feeling she did. She just didn't want to say it. He cleared his throat again, not knowing what to make of the question. "I'm not sure, actually. I've never really thought about it."

"I see." She nodded as her gaze dropped to the fire.

He could tell by her reaction that it hadn't been the answer she was looking for, and her disappointment piqued his curiosity.

"May I ask why you ask, Mrs. Jones?"

"Oh, no reason. It just seems out here . . . on the frontier and away from the civilization we were once from that . . . perhaps what we saw as proper is now twisted a little."

"I'm not sure I understand what you mean?"

"Well, like, the qualities of a woman that a young man wishes to marry. What might be shunned or not considered proper might not be the same out here or in Oregon as it is where we are from."

Heat rushed up the back of his neck, and he regretted asking a question for the first time. Of course, he wasn't a fool and had somewhat seen her answer coming. But still, knowing that is what she might say and hearing the words were two different things.

He cleared his throat for the third time. "I don't know what I think about that, Mrs. Jones. I suppose I shall have to figure it out when the time comes. For now, I'm just looking to get to Oregon. I have big plans for a business, and I need to see to that."

"Of course. I didn't mean anything by the questions. It's just something I've been thinking about. I don't know why." She laughed, and although he played along with her sudden change of mirth, a small part of him knew.

She was asking because of her daughter.

And she was asking him because of the same reason James had asked him about Lillian.

The only thing that he didn't know was why.

Had Lillian done something that would deem her unproper in the eyes of a man? And if so, what was it? He glanced at the young woman with her head still tucked toward her chest as she chopped the remaining potatoes, dumping them plus a chunk of chopped onion into the pan. She'd been nothing but a quiet, young lady around him, showing him nothing but kindness, and he didn't want to see her in a different light than the one he had.

"Do you need any help, Miss Jones," he asked her.

She glanced up at him and bit her lip, shaking her head. His eyes looked into hers, and he couldn't help but feel a sadness in her he hadn't ever felt before. It was as though she was hiding something painful that plagued her soul. It nudged at the depths of his guilt as though his indifference toward her mother's questions—although warranted in his mind—caused her more pain.

He hated the notion of it.

He thought of his own past and how he had a tarnished name in his hometown. He thought of the whispers behind his back and how no woman would have accepted his proposal, not after what his father had done and not after their family had lost everything. Had they stayed, it wouldn't have been just Emma whom their friends shunned.

It would have been him too.

"You know, Mrs. Jones, I'm not sure I would want a proper woman," he said, glancing back at Lillian's mother. "Sometimes people can't control their pasts. That doesn't mean they are bad people."

"You're right. It doesn't," she said, smiling. "I think I shall wake Mr. Jones now so he can enjoy breakfast with us."

FOUR

EVERETT

*E*verett didn't know what to make of the rest of breakfast. Although the subject of courting and marriage never came up again—and in fact, Mrs. Jones had become rather tight-lipped after Mr. Jones awoke—there was still the air around them that such things had been discussed.

Or at least broached.

And he didn't know how he felt about them.

He hadn't thought much about marriage since leaving Boston, figuring after he settled in Oregon, such things might cross his mind when God would mean for them to. He never thought about it while on the trail. There was far too much to look after, and although his sister wasn't one of those things anymore, he still didn't think he needed—or wanted—the distraction. Not to mention, he'd never thought about it when looking at any of the single women on the wagon train.

It wasn't that none of them were interesting or pretty. Lillian was—by his account—the prettiest of all his sister's friends, and although he didn't know much about her, she always seemed like a lovely young lady when she was in his company or he in hers.

Yes, there was nothing about her that should make him say no, and yet, still, he did.

Or does, he thought to himself. *I still do say no.*

But why?

He couldn't answer that.

And it drove him crazy.

"Did you have a nice breakfast?" a voice asked as he approached his wagon.

He spun to find Emma leaning against the wagon she shared with James. With a smile etched across her face, she cocked her head to the side.

It was a look he'd seen in her before when she was about to mock him for one thing or another. Usually, something he had done or was thinking of doing that she found funny or ironic, and it was always like a little knife she used to taunt him.

"I don't know what you're talking about." He made his way over to the buckets of water under the wagon. After grabbing one, he yanked his handkerchief from his back pocket and dunked the cloth in the water, letting it soak.

"Your breakfast with Mr. and Mrs. Jones. And Lillian, of course."

"What about it?"

"How was it? Did you have a nice time?"

"It was breakfast . . . on the trail. Something I've done I don't know how many times since we left Missouri. It wasn't like it was a special party or celebration."

"I know."

"You made it sound like it was, though."

Emma narrowed her eyes. "Don't be twisting my words so that you either confuse me or distract me from the conversation. I know what I asked. It doesn't have to be a party or celebration for you to have a nice time. All it takes is getting together with someone and having a conversation over a meal."

He inhaled a deep breath, grabbing the bridge of his nose as he exhaled. "Fine. Yes. It was an enjoyable time. They seem like nice and wonderful people."

"And Lillian?"

"What about her?"

"I just wondered if you spoke with her?"

"About?"

Emma glanced up at the sky, exhaling a deep breath. A slight growl vibrated through her chest. "You won't be able to do it, Everett."

"Do what?"

Her eyes narrowed again. "Distract me with your stupid, meaningless questions, going around and around them with your vague and ridiculous questions. I know what you are trying to do. Just stop."

"Stop what?"

"UGH!" She threw her hands in the air, clenching her fists before shaking them at him. "You are impossible."

"Well, if you're finished, then . . ." He paused but then spoke again before she could get a word in. "I'm exhausted, and I need to get some rest. I was out with the cattle all night and haven't had any sleep."

"Don't think you'll get out of this, Everett Michael Ford. You and I will talk about this."

"Did you just use my middle name like mother and father did when I was a boy?" He turned away from her, waving his hand. "And there's nothing to talk about Emma Renee Ford . . . Garrison. I need to get some rest."

"Everett, wait." Emma darted toward him, grabbing his arm. "I don't mean to upset you. I was just curious. Lillian is a lovely person. She's sweet and kind, and I just want to see you happy."

"And you think marriage will do that?"

"Well, I thought perhaps it would. I know it's made me happy. I know you had intentions with Emily Mae in Boston, and I know after . . . with what Father did . . . I just don't want you thinking you must shut your heart out to love and marriage because of what happened."

"I don't think that. I just have other things on my mind. Oregon. The business."

"I can understand that. I just didn't want you missing out on something that could be wonderful because you didn't think you deserved it . . . or needed it. Not that I'm saying you need love. But . . . well, hopefully, you know what I mean."

She offered him a smile, and he took a deep breath, letting his shoulders relax. "I do know what you mean. And thank you. I really need to get some rest."

"All right. We can talk later." She squeezed his arm and then headed off to her wagon.

He climbed in his, and although laying down for what felt like the first time in forever, there was a restlessness to his body. He laid on one side, blowing out several breaths as he tried to clear his mind of it all. Now wasn't the time to think of anything. Now was the time for sleep.

~

LILLIAN

*L*illian carried the bucket down to the river. The water inside sloshed, and the plates and cups from this morning's breakfast clanked together. While she could have washed up after the meal at the wagon, she also needed to get away.

It hadn't been the worst breakfast she'd ever had. Surely, there had been a time or two her mother had embarrassed her. Even with Jacob, her mother always seemed to ask questions she shouldn't. Or perhaps they were questions Lillian would have liked to ask but didn't have the courage. While she hoped it wasn't the latter, she couldn't help but feel it was. Her mother's boldness wasn't a quality she'd inherited, and at times she didn't know if that was a good thing or not.

She scrunched her face as she remembered her mother talking to Mr. Ford.

What he must think of her, she thought. *And the way my mother asked. Talking about proper women and women who weren't proper.*

"If he didn't think of me in a bad light already, he surely does now," she said aloud before biting her tongue and glancing around her, hoping no one was near to hear any of what she'd said.

That was all she needed to top off this glorious morning.

She rolled her eyes, heaving a deep breath as she adjusted the bucket in her hand and continued down to the water's edge.

"I was hoping I would find you," a voice said behind her as she knelt in the sand. She glanced over her shoulder to find Emma approaching her.

"Good morning."

"Good morning. Did you have a nice breakfast?" A smile spread on Emma's face.

"Not you too." Lillian shook her head, sighing as she reached into the bucket and grabbed a plate and the bar of soap sitting at the bottom. She lathered up her hands and scrubbed the plate, digging her nails into the food remains.

"And what is that supposed to mean?" Emma knelt beside her, holding out her hand as though silently offering to help her wash the dishes.

Lillian reached into the bucket, taking out another plate and handing it to her along with the bar of soap. "It means I have gotten enough questions from my mother about the situation."

"So, you admit there is a situation?" Emma glanced at her and winked.

"No. I don't admit there is a situation. Perhaps that was the wrong thing to say. I don't know how else to say it, though."

"And what do you think this situation is?"

"I don't know. I feel as though you and my parents are trying to force your brother and me together, and I don't know why."

"I wouldn't say force. I know I'm not forcing you." Emma rolled the bar of soap in her hand and scrubbed the plate while Lillian finished the plate in her hand and rinsed it in the river. With the dish soap-free, she laid her apron on the sand and set the plate on it to protect it from the sand.

"Well, perhaps you aren't, but my parents are. Or, actually, just my mother." Lillian grabbed another plate and the soap, repeating the process she'd done for the first one. Her movements jerked with her bubbling annoyance.

Emma watched her, and she raised one eyebrow. "May I ask you something?"

"All right."

"What is wrong with your mother's idea of you being with my brother? Is it because you don't think he is a good man? Because I assure you, he is. He's one of the best."

"No, it's not that I don't think he's a good man. It's just . . ." Lillian bit her lip. She knew this was a chance for her to tell Emma the truth about her late husband and the baby. The problem was, thinking of telling her friend everything and doing it were two different roads to take, and she wasn't sure she dared to take the one she knew she should, especially when the other road of not telling her was so much easier.

"What is it then?" Emma stared at her with her brow creased with concern, and when Lillian didn't say anything, she continued her thought. "Is it because of our past?"

"Your past? What are you talking about?"

Emma inhaled a deep breath, letting it out slowly. "So, you don't know?"

"Know what?"

"I thought perhaps he had told you or something."

"Told me what?"

"We had to leave Boston because of my father. He made a

few bad business deals, and my family lost everything. No man would dare take my hand in marriage, and no woman would even look in Everett's direction. The family name is tarnished."

"I didn't know, and I'm sorry to hear about that. It must have been awful to have to leave everything along with your family."

"It was. But I think it will work out for the better. I felt he wouldn't want you to know that, but I suppose I had to make sure he didn't tell you."

"No, he didn't. And it's not because of that. Such things wouldn't even matter to me. Family names and social status are not where I came from, nor would I want to be. Not that there is anything wrong with people who want those things." Lillian's gaze widened as she hoped she didn't offend Emma.

Emma smiled and rested her wet hand on Lillian's shoulder as if to calm Lillian's concerns. "I understand what you meant." Emma finished washing the plate, and after rinsing it, she handed it back to Lillian. "So, if that isn't the reason, why don't you want to entertain the idea of my brother?"

Lillian inhaled and exhaled a deep breath. Her honesty sat on the tip of her tongue, and yet, no matter how much she wanted to give the words liberty, she couldn't. "It just doesn't seem like the right time. He seems to have goals and dreams and is focused on those."

"Well, yes, he does. But I think that deep down, he thinks about the notions of love and marriage."

"If he did, if they were what he wanted, he would find them. He doesn't act as though he has, and until he chooses . . ." Lillian paused as she glanced at her friend. "If we were meant to be together, then you and my parents wouldn't have to work so hard to make it happen."

Emma opened her mouth but closed it without saying a word.

It was about the best reason Lillian could give at that moment, and the only thing she could do was thank God for giving her the exact words to say. Even though she had only meant them to be an excuse to stop her friend from pushing the subject further, she couldn't deny how much validity they held.

It was true, after all, she thought.

If Everett were meant for her, there wouldn't be any obstacles.

Period.

FIVE

LILLIAN

*L*illian had heard Mr. Russell speak of Fort Laramie for the last twenty miles. He called it the Crossroads to the West, and while she hadn't understood exactly what he meant, she could a little more as the Fort came into view.

The fort was alive with movement. Wagons rolled in all directions while men rode horses, herding cattle east, west, north, and south and women and children walked alongside the wagons, some followed by dogs, others by goats. Horses neighed, cows mooed, and the dogs and goats barked and bleated. The goats' huge milk-filled udders swung from side to side as the animals trotted alongside their owners.

Lillian's father followed the wagon before him, driving down toward the fort and passing several onlookers who had set up camp. Men, women, and children either tended to the chores, chopping up the deer that laid across the table, hanging the laundry on the line, or sitting by the campfire with a pot of steaming food on the fire and plates in their laps. No matter what age they were, they all watched as the wagons passed. A few of the children even waved. Lillian waved back.

As they drew near the entrance to the fort, Mr. Russell signaled everyone to circle up, and Lillian's father turned the horses and followed the wagon in front of them until he pulled the horse team to a stop and jumped down. The rest of the men in the wagon train did the same, and as Mr. Ford rounded his wagon, Lillian glanced up at him.

Their eyes met, and her stomach fluttered as he smiled and tipped his hat at her.

While she had spent the better part of the last two days riding in the wagon and thinking about all the reasons why they couldn't—or shouldn't—be together, she had also spent time thinking about how it would feel to be in love again. Although she knew it would be weird to feel another man's arms around her or another man's lips on hers, she also couldn't deny how much she missed it and how much it gutted her when her husband died.

"Lillian?" her mother asked, distracting her. "Do you think you can head into the fort to buy the supplies we need?"

"Of course. What do you wish for me to buy?"

Her mother prattled off a list as Lillian glanced at Mr. Ford again. While her mother had stolen her attention from his, he had moved on to getting his wagon settled and his horses unhitched, and she watched him as he led the animals away from the circle toward the river to give them a much-needed drink.

"Did you hear me? Lillian? Lillian!"

Her mother's voice caused her to flinch. "What?"

"I asked if you heard me." Her mother rested her hand on her hip as she cocked her head to the side.

"I'm sorry, Mother, but I didn't."

"That's what I thought. Honestly, child, you need to pay attention." Her mother waved at her to get down from the buckboard. "Do you need me to find a piece of paper and a pencil and write everything down?"

"No, Mother. I'll remember. What is it you wish for me to buy?"

While her mother prattled off the list again, Lillian paid attention, making a mental note of each thing before she took the money from her mother's hand and headed toward the other wagons to see if Emma, Abby, Sadie, and Charlotte wanted to go to the fort with her.

~

*A*rmed with the mental list from her mother and with the money stuffed in her belt, Lillian made her way through the crowded supply tents in the fort. Emma and Abby had accompanied her while Sadie and Charlotte had to see to chores before they even thought about what they needed to buy. But they wished the other girls well as they waved from the wagons.

"Where should we start?" Abby asked as she lifted her hand to her forehead to shield the sun from her eyes. "William said we need flour and beans, so . . ." She glanced around at the different tents, squinting.

"I think most of them will have the supplies we need." Emma moved over to one tent and lifted the flap, peeking inside. She waved the two women over. "This one is interesting."

She opened the flap, and the three walked inside. Shelves lined three sides of the tent, while tables were set up in the middle. While this tent lacked any of the food supplies the women needed, the odds and ends in this place piqued their attention, and as Emma and Abby moved to the other side of the tent, Lillian stopped and stared at one shelf. Different pots and pans were stacked on the bottom while the middle held different sizes of coffee kettles, ladles, and spatulas. The shelf above held plates, cups, and different-sized knives. The blades all glinted in the little sunlight that filtered through a hole in the roof of the tent.

She leaned in, looking at the different shaped handles. Each one looked hand carved.

"Never thought of you as one to be interested in knives," a voice said behind her.

She spun, nearly knocking into Mr. Ford as her haste caused her balance to wobble, and Mr. Ford held out his arm to help her. She grabbed him and steadied herself.

"I'm sorry for startling you," he said.

"It's all right. I just moved too quickly." She let go of his arm, clearing her throat as she stepped away from him a couple of steps. Her gaze dropped to the ground.

"They are interesting, though." He pointed toward the knives. "Aren't they?"

"Yes, I suppose they are. I was just looking at the handles." She didn't want to think about how Jacob had always held an interest in knives. He'd even made a couple by carving the handles and forging the blades.

"I've always wondered how they do that."

"It's mainly with a knife." The words left her mouth, and she covered it with her hand for a moment, clearing her throat again. "Or I assume it is. I don't know."

"No, I think you're right." He picked one up, flipping it over in his hand. "I think I like this one the best." He held it out for her to take. She didn't take it but touched it, letting her fingertips graze over the oak handle. The wood had several shades of brown running through it with a knot on one side.

"It's pretty. I think I like it too . . . the best, I mean. I like it the best too."

He tried to hand it to her again. "Do you want to buy it?"

Heat flushed through her cheeks. "Oh, no. I don't need it."

"Are you sure?"

"Yes. I'm just here for flour, beans, cornmeal, salt, and bacon."

"Those are all over in another tent. Do you want me to show you the way?"

She bit her lip and glanced over to Emma and Abby, who were still standing on the other side of the tent. Both women were staring at Lillian and Mr. Ford. Emma had a broad grin etched across her face.

"You can show us the way," Lillian said.

Mr. Ford's face turned slightly pink, and he ducked his chin. "Of course. I'd be happy to help."

He led the three women to another tent, and as they entered, Lillian could smell the stored food from inside the sacks. Her stomach twisted a little at all the scents, and she covered her mouth for a second, closing her eyes as she prayed she wouldn't get sick.

Not here, she thought. Not now.

"Are you all right?" Emma asked her.

"Fine. I'm just . . . there are a lot of supplies here. I'm thankful we will find everything we need."

Emma raised one eyebrow, giving her an odd look of hesitation. "Yes, I suppose that is helpful."

While Emma and Abby meandered through the tent, stopping and checking out different stacks of supplies, Lillian followed Mr. Ford around to the other side, and she watched as he pointed everything out.

"Do you have a list written down?" he asked, motioning her to follow him toward a man standing behind a desk-like table.

"No. It's all in my head."

As they reached the table, the man tipped his hat and smiled. "Good day to you both. How can I help you today?"

"This young woman would like to order some supplies," Mr. Ford hooked his thumb toward Lillian, and the man nodded. "All right. What can I get for you, ma'am?"

She gave him the list, waiting between telling him each thing while he jotted them all down on a scrap of paper. His chicken-scratch handwriting was hard to read upside down.

"So, do you have it all?" she asked when she was finished.

"Yes, ma'am, I do. It will be five dollars."

She handed him the money, and he grabbed it and stuffed it in his pocket. "Do you want to take it all now?"

"Now?" Heat rushed up through the back of her neck. She hadn't thought about how she would get the supplies back through the fort and down to her wagon.

"May I pick up the supplies later when I come for mine?" Mr. Ford asked.

"Of course." The man jotted his signature on the slip of paper. "Just bring that with ya when you come back."

"Thank you."

As the man wandered off to help another couple looking to purchase what they needed, Mr. Ford stuffed the piece of paper in his pocket and shrugged.

"I hope it's all right with you that I come to get them later. I figured it would be easier," he said.

"Of course, it's all right, Mr. Ford. And it would be easier. For a moment there, I was worried about how I would get all the things back to the wagon." Lillian laughed slightly as she brushed her forehead with her fingers.

"You can call me Everett, Miss Jones. There's no sense in being formal. Not anymore, or at least I think."

"I suppose you're right."

"So, does that mean I may call you Lillian?"

Her name on his lips was like a gentle breeze against her ears, and the way it rolled off his tongue . . .

It was the first time she ever loved her name and the first time she loved the sound of it.

"Of course."

"Anyway, I figure I'll make a travois that I can tie to one of the horses, or I'll bring my wagon up here. I should probably let Emma and Abby know so I can get theirs too." He motioned for Lillian to follow him, and they both made their way over to the other side of the tent, where the woman stood near a shelf looking at different trinkets.

"I remember having one of these," Emma said, holding up a silver mirror. "I wish I would have brought it. Look, Everett, isn't it lovely?"

"I suppose it is if you like those types of things."

She furrowed her brow at him. "Oh, hush. It's lovely, and you know it."

He smiled. "If you say so."

"Oh, look at this," Emma gushed as she lunged forward and grabbed a blue knit blanket from the bottom shelf. "It's just precious." She unfolded the blanket, holding it up to reveal its small size.

"That thing wouldn't keep anyone warm," Mr. Ford said with a slight chuckle in his chest.

"It's not for an adult, you fool. It's for a baby." She turned away from her brother, holding it up in front of Abby. "Perhaps you should buy it."

Abby's mouth gaped open. "Why on earth would you show me that? I'm not with child."

Emma winked. "Yet."

Abby grabbed the blanket and waved it in front of Emma's face, taunting her with it in the same manner in which Emma taunted Abby. "Well, I could say the same to you, too."

Emma let out a shriek. "Not in front of my brother." She stole the blanket back and then waved it in front of him. "Perhaps you want it."

"Yes, because out of the four of us, I will need it the most."

"You never know what the future holds, dear brother." Emma shrugged and then winked at him before she looked at

Lillian. "What do you think, Lillian? It's a lovely shade of blue, don't you think?"

A lump formed in Lillian's throat, and although she fought them off, tears threatened to mist her eyes. She didn't know what to say, nor did she know if she could even speak, and she bit her lip, ducking her chin against her chest. Out of the three women, she was the one who would need the blanket, and yet no one could know.

Especially the man standing next to her.

"I think I should go," she said, darting for the flap of the tent.

Although the women called after her, she ignored them, and as the sun shined on her face outside, she inhaled a deep breath and closed her eyes.

"Lillian?" Mr. Ford called out, following her outside. "Lillian? Are you all right?"

"Yes, of course. I'm sorry to rush off as I did. But I should be getting back to the wagon. I'm sure my parents are expecting me."

"I can walk you back there. If you want."

"Oh no, that's not necessary. You've already done so much for me today. Thank you for the help with the supplies this afternoon. Please let my father know when you plan on coming back for the supplies. I'm sure he will wish to help."

"I will do that."

"And please let Emma and Abby know I will see them later."

"I will do that too."

Without another word, she spun and headed back to the wagons, fighting off tears with every step.

SIX

EVERETT

*E*verett watched as Lillian darted off through the crowd of the fort. A slight twinge of guilt hit his chest, and he didn't know why. He hadn't done anything wrong, or at least he hadn't thought he did. Perhaps it wasn't guilt. Perhaps it was annoyance in his sister for what she'd done. She'd obviously upset Lillian, yet he didn't know why or how.

He marched back into the supply tent, finding Emma and Abby still looking through the different shelves for odds and ends.

"And what was that all about?" he asked his sister. His voice had a curter tone than he'd planned, but he didn't regret it.

"What are you talking about?" Emma turned toward him; her eyes widened a little, but then, taking notice of his tone, she furrowed her brow. "And what has got your tail in a tizzy?"

"You upset her."

"Oh, I did not. She's just shy like that."

"Are you sure about that?"

Emma rested her hand on her hip. "Everett, I think I know the type of woman Lillian is. I've only been her friend for months. She's quiet, and sometimes, she just leaves the conversation without a word to anyone. It's just how she is."

"I don't think you're right on this one. She looked upset."

"Well, I don't know why. I didn't do or say anything."

"Again, I have to ask if you're sure about that."

Emma opened her mouth but closed it, letting out a sigh. "Yes, I'm fairly certain."

Everett glanced at Abby as though silently asking her if she agreed with him or Emma. Abby shrugged and shook her head slightly before walking off to leave the sparring siblings to their conversation. For a moment, Everett envied her ability to leave without concerning herself over the matter.

This was why he never got involved with the affairs of his sister's friends back home. He never liked the drama that came with the young ladies or the gossip. He wanted a simple woman, one who was just happy with life and content in knowing that her business was hers and hers alone. She didn't need to involve herself in another life.

"If you wish for me to, I will talk to her, but I don't think you are warranted in any concern." Emma waved her hand before moving around him and making her way over to another shelf. She grabbed the silver mirror again, looking at it for a moment before something else seemed to catch her attention. She squealed. "Abby! It has a matching brush."

~

*A*lthough Everett tried to forget about the morning and not only what his sister had done but what she had said, it was all he thought about as he constructed the travois and hooked it to his horse. There was something about Lillian that he just couldn't put his finger on, and while part of that notion scared him a little—as he wasn't sure if the something was a good thing or a bad thing—it also piqued his interest even more in the woman.

She was kind, lovely, and quiet. Three qualities that would lead someone to believe that there was nothing a person like that could do wrong. It wasn't like a kind person would murder someone, or a lovely person would cheat or swindle someone out of money or possessions. It also wasn't like an otherwise quiet person would cause a drunken scene or act in a vulgar unladylike manner.

So, what was it that seemed to cause her so much bother?

The question went round and round his mind so often that he almost felt dizzy. He wanted to know the answer yet didn't want to pry. It was her business, after all, and none of his. It wasn't as though he was courting the woman. He didn't have any intentions at all.

Or did he?

No, he thought to himself. *Don't question that. Why would I question that? I do not have intentions with Lillian. Not at all.*

A slight groan left his lips with his thoughts. He hadn't seen them coming, and for them to pop up in the manner they did . . . well, it knocked his senses a little off balance.

He shook his head, grabbing the horse's lead as he headed toward the fort to gather the supplies he purchased and to pick up the ones for Mr. and Mrs. Ford.

And for Lillian, he thought, groaning again as the little voice inside his head seemed to smile at the mention of her name. *What on earth was wrong with him?*

Heat prickled against his neck as he made his way through the gates of the fort and toward the tent. The morning sunlight from a few hours ago had hardened into the afternoon glare that beat down on him, causing a thin layer of sweat to form on his forehead. He tried to wipe it away, but the relentlessness of it only plagued him more. There was nothing wrong with Wyoming, and it had a lot of good qualities about it, but he was ready to move on, ready to see the mountains and forests. He longed for cool air—or at least some shade—and as he tied the horse to the tie post in front of the supply tent, his throat begged for water.

"Oh, come on, darlin'. Aren't ya going to even let me help?" a male's voice said.

A few other men laughed with the one talking, and as Everett was about to open the flap of the supply tent, he glanced over, catching sight of Lillian struggling with a sack of flour while three men watched her.

"We told you we'd help you," one of the other men said as he moved toward her and tried to grab the sack from her.

Lillian cringed. Her grip tightened on the bag, and she jerked it around, trying to get the man to release it. "I don't need your help." She continued to rip it from his grasp, and he released it; she dropped it in the dirt.

The three men laughed.

"Now, you see what you've done?" the man said, pointing toward the sack. "If you'd let me help you, that wouldn't have happened." He kicked the sack, and she moved over to it, trying to block it from him.

"I said I don't need your help," she said again.

"Are you sure about that?" the third man said through his mirth.

A flicker of anger bubbled in Everett's chest, and he clenched his fists as he marched over to the scene. "You heard the lady," he said to the men. A hard growl vibrated through his tone. "She said she didn't need your help."

"And just what are you going to do about it?" the first man asked. He squared his chest and brushed his jacket away from his waist, exposing the gun holstered on his hip.

Everett's eyes narrowed. He didn't want to be in another gunfight. Not after the one at Fort Kearney and at the bandit's camp any more than he wanted to poke his own eyes out with a spoon. But it didn't matter what he didn't want. It only mattered that the men leave Lillian alone.

"Is that supposed to intimidate me?" Everett asked, stepping closer to the man.

Lillian gasped, and a few other women walking past noticed the two men and the exposed gun screamed and ran. Their fear caught the attention of a few other men sitting in front of a nearby tent, who studied the scene for a moment before rising to their feet and making their way over.

"Is there a problem going on?" one of them asked.

The three men glanced at the newcomer, and while it seemed at first that they would give him a smart-mouthed answer, their eyes widened, and they shook their heads. "No, sir, Mr. Kelly," each of them said, and they all lifted their hands, turned, and darted away without looking over their shoulders.

Everett heaved a sigh, turning to Lillian, who stood next to him with her hand covering her mouth. He had an over-whelming need to wrap his arms around her and hug her, but he clasped his hands behind his back to stop himself. He didn't want to do anything she wasn't comfortable with. He also didn't want to scare her more than she already was.

"Are you all right?" he asked.

She glanced from him to the man who seemed to strike fear in the other three men. "Yes." She turned toward the one they called Mr. Kelly. "Thank you. I'm sorry to have been a bother."

"You weren't, ma'am." He tipped his hat and opened his jacket, showing her a badge. "It's my job to keep those who wish to flirt with the law in check." Before she could say another word, he nodded and turned, walking away from them as he pulled his hat further down his eyes.

Everett and Lillian watched him until Lillian bent down, reaching for the sack of flour. Everett blocked her grasp and grabbed the sack before she could get it.

"Where are you taking this?" he asked her.

"To the wagon."

"But I told you I would get it with my supplies and bring it to you."

"I know you did. I just . . . I just didn't want to be a bother."

"If I thought it would have been a bother, I wouldn't have offered." He smiled and motioned her to follow him back to his horse tied outside the supply tent.

She did.

"What were you thinking you were going to do?" he asked as he threw the sack down on the travois. "Just take everything down on different trips?"

"No. My father is here. We were going to carry everything together. I just thought I would get a head start with the flour."

"Your father?" Everett spun in a circle, looking for Mr. Jones. "Where is he?"

"He's inside, talking to the man with the supplies."

At the mention of her father, Mr. Jones came out from the tent. He smiled as he noticed his daughter and Everett, and he blinked as though a slight hint of relief warmed through him. "Ah. Mr. Ford. Good to see you."

"You too, Mr. Jones."

The men shook hands.

"I see you have our sack of flour." Mr. Jones pointed toward the travois.

"Yes, I saw Lillian struggling with the sack—"

"I wasn't struggling that much."

Everett gave her a sideways glance with her interruption. "I saw Lillian carrying the sack and thought, why not help? I had offered to help earlier when she ordered the supplies."

"You did?" Mr. Jones looked at his daughter, but she ducked her chin as though she was trying to hide her face from him.

Everett cleared his throat. "Perhaps I didn't make myself clear. I tend to do that from time to time."

Lillian looked up, meeting his gaze for a moment.

"Well, you're here now, and that's all that matters. Shall we get all the other supplies?" Mr. Jones hooked his thumb over his shoulder, and as Everett made his way into the tent, Mr. Jones followed.

"I'm sure glad you came up here. I was not looking forward to carrying all those supplies back to the wagon."

SEVEN

LILLIAN

*L*illian had watched Everett with the supplies that afternoon, watched how he'd taken the time to load them with care, talk with her father while they took them back to the wagons, and how he'd unloaded them. It was hard to see him work and not think about the type of man he was. She didn't want heartbreak, regret, or disappointment, and as she felt the tug on her heartstrings, the more she knew she could travel down a dangerous road if she'd let herself.

And she couldn't do that.

Knowing this, she forced herself to stay away the rest of the time they were at Fort Laramie, mainly keeping to herself and even staying away from the other women—something they noticed. Still, no matter how often they asked her to come with them to bathe or wash their clothes, she stayed near her wagon, tending to any chore she could do alone.

"You've been quiet," her mother said as the wagon rolled down the trail. They'd left the Fort the day before, heading out in the early morning hours, much to Lillian's relief. Traveling meant she would have the distraction she needed. Traveling meant she wouldn't have to talk to anyone.

Well, almost.

She still had her mother to contend with while her father rode alongside the wagon.

"I didn't know I was," she lied, hoping her mother would let the conversation die.

"Is something the matter?"

What wasn't, she thought. Did Mother want the list of all the wrong things?

"No. I'm just tired."

"I can understand that. Have you spoken to Mr. Ford?"

"No."

Her mother glanced at her. "Oh. I thought you would have. When was the last time you did?"

"I don't know. I think the day he brought the supplies to the wagon."

"Lillian, that was two days ago."

"So?"

"So, don't you think you should have spoken with him in those two days?"

"No, I don't. He's just a man on this wagon train, Mother. Nothing more."

She closed her eyes, praying her mother would let the conversation end. She knew all the different directions it could take, and she didn't like them.

"I think he likes you."

And there it was. The one direction the conversation could go that she feared the most.

"Mother, please, don't say things like that."

"Why wouldn't I? It's the truth. I think he does."

"It doesn't matter if he does or doesn't. He won't, when he finds out the truth."

"I know you keep saying that, but I get the feeling he's not like that. I don't think he will care, and I think if you just told him, you would see it too."

"I'm not going to tell him."

Mother opened her mouth, but before she could say a word, they both heard a crack, and the wagon lurched then the back of it collapsed. The jolt sent Lillian backward, and she screamed as her legs flew in the air. Her head jerked, and pain shot down her neck as she scrambled and grabbed the buckboard. Her grip was so tight that her knuckles turned white. Her mother also fell backward, and she jerked the reins, holding on to them to keep her from tumbling out of the wagon as it swayed from side to side, threatening to tip over as it fishtailed through the dirt. The wooden sides cracked and moaned, and the canvas bonnet shook, tearing in the corner.

The pressure of the wagon's back end hitting the ground lifted the harnesses, and the horses bolted forward, hitting the ends of the leather straps. The sudden jerked movement caused the wagon to lurch again, and the front bumped into the hindquarters of the back horses, which sent them into the lead horses, and all four animals panicked a second time; this time, they took off at a gallop, dragging the wagon behind them.

Lillian and her mother both screamed, and as Lillian glanced over, she saw her father's horse galloping alongside the wagon. She reached out to him, but instead of grabbing on to her, he cued his horse to go fast, passing the wagon as he headed for the wagon horses. The front wheels continued down the trail, hitting a rock that sent the wagon bouncing. Although Lillian tried to hang on, her fingers slipped from the buckboard, and she fell to the ground, rolling several times before landing on her stomach. She turned her head, watching the wagon continue without her as the backend dragged in the dirt. A huge cloud of dust enveloped her, and the dirt burned her eyes and nose. She coughed and sputtered as she struggled to her feet. Several more horses ran past her as Mr. Russell, the cowboys, Mr. Garrison, and Mr. Campbell ran after the out-of-control wagon and her father.

"Lillian! Lillian!" Everett shouted as he galloped his horse toward her, jerking it to a halt before he jumped off and lunged for her. His hands slid up her cheeks, and his face was inches from hers. His lungs heaved. "Are you all right?"

She nodded, and although she opened her mouth to speak, nothing came out.

"Are you sure?" he asked.

She nodded again, then glanced in the direction the wagon disappeared.

"Lillian!" Emma shouted as she approached. Abby, Sadie, and Charlotte hurried along with her, and they all wrapped their arms around her when they reached her.

"Get her to my wagon," Everett told Emma.

Before she could agree or disagree, he climbed back on his horse and spurred it to run after the rest.

"Lillian, are you hurt?" Sadie asked. She grabbed Lillian's face, looking at her eyes. "Does anything hurt?"

"Falling out of the wagon didn't feel too good."

It was the only thing she could think to say and the only words she could get out of her mouth.

"I think she'll be all right," Charlotte said with a slight chuckle in her voice.

Sadie gave her a sideways glare, then focused on Lillian again. "I realize that falling out of the wagon didn't feel good. But do you have any pain anywhere? Can you move everything?" Without waiting for an answer, she grabbed Lillian's arms, bending them and moving them in all directions. "Can you turn your head?" She moved Lillian's head. "And can you walk?" She stepped away from Lillian but grabbed Lillian's hands to direct Lillian to follow. After she walked around her, prodding a few other areas of Lillian's body, she smiled. "I think Charlotte's right. I think you'll be all right."

As the women began walking Lillian to Everett's wagon, Mr.

Russell and a few of the other men returned. "Let's get the wagons moved out."

"Where are my parents?" Lillian asked him.

"About a quarter of a mile down the trail. We got the horses stopped, but the wagon is in bad shape. Your mother and father are all right. Just a little shaken."

While Emma climbed into her wagon, Lillian and Sadie climbed into Everett's, and they all followed the rest of the wagon train down the trail until they came upon the broken wagon Lillian had called home for the last couple of months. The sight of its mangled bonnet and broken sides caused her to cover her mouth with her hand, and she climbed down from Everett's wagon, running toward her parents, who were standing next to the crash. The three hugged.

"Are you all right?" she asked her mother.

"Of course. Just a little rattled. That's all."

"What happened?"

"From the looks of it, both back wheels broke off. I don't know what happened to them or why. But it spooked the horses." Her father wrapped one arm around his wife, squeezing her as he kissed her head. His eyes were still wide, and he still breathed heavy.

She glanced from her parents to the wreck of a wagon, watching Mr. Garrison, Mr. Campbell, and Everett as they walked around the wagon, inspecting different parts of it. They talked to each other in a hushed, mumbled tone that Lillian couldn't hear.

"Can we fix it?"

She stepped toward the three men, and as she did, Everett glanced over his shoulder. His brow furrowed, and he looked at the ground for a moment before looking at her again and shaking his head.

Her mother cried behind her, and she heard her father

patting her mother's shoulder. "It will be all right, Margaret. We'll figure something out."

"But what are we going to do, Harold?" her mother asked. "We can't carry all our things. Our belongings. Our supplies."

"We can try to find another wagon at the next outpost."

"But we can't afford it. We only have a little money left, and that is supposed to help us get a start in Oregon." She sobbed even harder, and Lillian's stomach clenched. She turned and glanced back in the direction they came, back to Fort Laramie. Surely, it was close enough that they could return on foot or horseback. But that didn't solve the problem of money.

Why did all the problems have to be around money?

She wanted to hate it, and yet she knew it was foolish to do so.

Money wasn't the problem. Money didn't make Jacob borrow it, nor did it cause the accident.

"You're more than welcome to my wagon." Everett made his way toward Lillian's parents, repeating his words as he removed the hat from his head.

"That's kind of you, Mr. Ford, but what will you do?"

"Well, I figure, I'm riding and helping take care of the cattle so much that I don't need a wagon. It's become somewhat of a hindrance, anyway, always having to worry about driving it when I'd rather be in the saddle. Plus, we can hook your horses to it, which gives it another team, and they should be able to pull it with the weight of your supplies and mine. I think it could work."

"Are you sure our wagon can't be fixed?" Lillian asked him.

She didn't want to sound ungrateful for his offer, but the thought of them now traveling together, along with all the feelings that she'd been fighting when it came to the likes of Everett Ford, suddenly pounded down upon her. The weight of it nearly made her struggle to breathe. Of course, she wanted to be near him. She longed for it. But she also knew she shouldn't.

"I don't think so." He turned away from them. "James? William? Can you fix it?"

Both the men shook their heads, and Lillian's stomach twisted even more.

"You're more than welcome to my offer."

Before she could open her mouth to say no, her parents stepped forward, shaking Everett's hand. "Thank you so much. We're so grateful for your kind offer," her father said.

"And I want you to know you won't have to worry about any meals. You'll be eating with us for the rest of our travels."

Everett chuckled, dropping his gaze to the ground before looking back at her mother. "That's kind of you, Mrs. Jones. Thank you."

Her mother turned toward her. "Lillian? Isn't it such a wonderful blessing?" her mother gushed.

Lillian nodded, looking into Everett's eyes. Her heart skipped a beat. She was in trouble. So much trouble she didn't know what she would do.

"Yes," she said, dropping her voice to a whisper. "It's a huge blessing."

EIGHT

EVERETT

"*I* don't know what you were thinking." Emma shook her head as she watched Everett fold his blankets and toss them on the log next to the campfire.

He'd spent the better part of the late afternoon and early evening reorganizing his wagon to make room for the Jones' belongings, and as the sky began to darken, he'd finally made enough room even if he had to store a few things in James' and Emma's wagon, which he was now packing. It wasn't much, just a few things he was sure they didn't mind.

At least, he thought they wouldn't.

"I thought that they needed help, and I was able to give it to them. Do you want me to move my things to William and Abby's wagon? They said they would help?" He pointed toward the blankets and the extra wagon wheel he'd moved over to their camp.

"No. No. You are more than welcome to leave it with us. I was just wondering why. I thought you didn't have intentions with Lillian."

"So, in order to help her family, I have to have intentions for her?"

"No. I guess I don't mean that either. I don't know. It just seemed . . ."

"Seemed like what?"

"You two have just been together a lot lately. It feels like there might be some feeling between you two. Not that there is anything wrong with that." Emma folded her arms across her chest and her brow furrowed.

"So, what seems to be the problem then?" He cocked his head to the side, giving her a wide smile. He didn't know why her feathers were ruffled, but he couldn't help but find amusement in it.

She inhaled a deep breath as she looked up at the sky. "I don't know. I just don't want you to give up all these things."

"What things am I giving up?"

Emma closed her eyes for a moment and then inhaled a breath, letting it out slowly as she looked at him. "You know, never mind anything I've said. Mr. and Mrs. Jones are lovely people, and Lillian . . . well, she is about the closest thing to a sister I have aside from Abby, and if you want to help them the only way you know how . . . I think you are nothing short of the amazing man you've always been."

He smiled again, winking at her. "When was I not that?"

She slapped his arm, and he laughed.

"Are you staying for supper?" she asked.

"Not tonight. Mrs. Jones insisted I share a meal with them, and I have to check on Willy and Beau first to make sure they don't need me for tonight. I'm kind of hoping they do. I wouldn't mind another night out in the field. It's peaceful."

"My brother, the sudden cowboy. Since when did you want to stay up all night watching cattle?" She chuckled and shook her head.

"I know. Sometimes I wonder what father and mother would think of it all. But then I think that I don't really want to know."

Although a smile hinted throughout her face, Emma lost a little of her amusement, and a frown curved through her lips. "I do the same thing. Like I wonder how they would feel knowing I married a soldier. Would they think it was wonderful, or would they not?"

"Do you think you'll write to them when you get to Oregon?"

She bit her lip for a second and shook her head. "I'm not sure. Perhaps I might let them know what has happened. Part of me doesn't wish to tell them where we are, yet I feel guilty for saying that and even thinking of it. They should know where their children are and what happened to them. I would want to know. I don't have children yet, but I can imagine how hard it would be for them to leave, and not only would I never see them again, but I'd never hear from them. Seems cruel."

"I've thought the same."

"I asked Pastor Smith about it."

"You did?"

"Well, I asked him about forgiving people as God has forgiven us. It's hard for me to hold anger toward them for what they've done when I am not without sin, and God has forgiven me."

"And what did he say?"

"Just that. I know I need to forgive them, and one of the things that helps me is when I look at James. I think of Edward and the kind of life I would have had. It wouldn't have been what I wanted. I probably would have thought it was because I didn't know any different."

"That's how I feel about being out with the cattle."

"Ah." She threw her head back a little as she laughed. "Now I understand." She paused briefly, nodding as though she agreed with her inner thoughts. "Perhaps when we get to Oregon, we will write them. We don't have to tell them everything, but we will write them."

"All right."

Tears slightly misted her eyes, and she waved her hand. "Now, off with you. Check on the cattle and enjoy your supper. I can imagine Mrs. Jones is already prepared to talk your ears off."

"I know. I don't think I mind, though."

"Well, that's probably a good thing."

~

*A*fter securing that Willy and Beau were fine for the evening, Everett made his way back to his wagon. Mrs. Jones had already set up the campsite, complete with having a fire going, and her pot hung above the flames. The stew inside bubbled as steam rose in the air. It smelled good. Really good. And his stomach growled as he sat on the log and scooped up a spoonful of water from the bucket.

"I hope you're hungry, Mr. Ford," Mrs. Jones said. She stood near the back of the wagon, dusting biscuits in the cornmeal before laying them in the pan.

"I am." He waited for her to walk over to the fire and smiled. "And, you're more than welcome to call me Everett, Ma'am."

She smiled and nodded. "All right. Well, I'm Margret, and my husband is Samuel." She bent down and placed the pan on the fire. "Supper should be done soon."

"Well, it smells delicious. I'm afraid I'm not much of a cook, so I haven't been eating much since Emma was married."

"That's all going to change now." She wiggled her finger at him and straightened up. "Lillian should be back any moment. She went to go fetch some water."

He glanced over his shoulder toward the creek, knowing how far the walk was and how heavy a bucket of water could be. A slight bit of longing twisted in his stomach, and he rose to his feet.

"I think I'll go help her."

Margaret smiled again. "I'm sure she would like that."

It wasn't long before Everett found Lillian down by the water. With the bucket filled, she had turned and started up the riverbank, slipping a little in the deep sand. He reached out, grabbing her arm.

She flinched and jerked it away.

"I'm sorry. I didn't mean to startle you." He offered his hand again, and this time, she took it.

"It's all right."

"I seem to do that a lot lately. Hopefully, there will come a time when I won't."

"Considering how jumpy I've been while on this trip, I'm afraid that might not be the case until we reach Oregon." She chuckled at her words, and her shoulders softened. "What can I do for you?" she asked.

He stuck out his hand again, motioning for the bucket. "Nothing. I came to help you."

"Thank you."

After taking the bucket from her, he walked alongside her as they made their way back to the wagons. The late afternoon heat had begun to cool, and while the birds chirped less as they drifted back to their nests for the night, the frogs and crickets seemed to come alive, especially down by the creek.

"Are you feeling all right?" he asked, glancing at her as they meandered through the tall grass.

"I'm a little sore, but otherwise all right."

"I can't imagine how scary that was."

"It is not something I wish to live through again. It reminded me of when Abby fell out of the wagon in the river. Although I didn't fall into the water, I know how she must have felt."

"I almost had forgotten about that."

"I know. Me too."

They walked a bit in silence before Lillian cleared her throat.

"It was kind of you to share your wagon. I don't know what we would have done if you hadn't offered."

"I'm sure your parents would have figured out something."

"Perhaps. Although, I hate to say it, part of me wonders if they would have. It's not like there were a lot of options for us."

"Well, it's over and done with now. You're on your way to Oregon, and we still have another fort and outpost before we reach Idaho. It will all work out."

While he didn't know who had slowed down first, they both seemed to take each step as though they wanted the walk to the wagon to last, and he couldn't help but smile to himself.

"I went to check on the cattle before I stopped by the wagons. They seem to be doing all right," he said, unsure of why he felt the need to bring up a herd of bovines, and yet, there was a part of him who needed the little bit of distraction.

"Do you like looking after them?" she asked.

He shrugged. "I do. It's interesting. Plus, it gives me something to do. Something to look forward to. I never thought of myself as a cowboy, but I kind of like it."

"What did you think you would do? I mean for work?"

"I had always thought I would work with my father. When that fell through, the only thing I could think about was opening up a general store. I knew I couldn't do it in Boston, though."

"I'm sorry to hear that."

"I don't think it bothers me that I couldn't. I was never attached to the notion of staying in the city. Of course, I never dreamed of all of this," he outstretched the arm not carrying the bucket and motioned to the prairie around them, "but I knew the city . . . it just wasn't for me."

"It must be nice to know those things when so many young men don't."

"I suppose it is." He chuckled slightly as it dawned on him that it was only because of his father's bad business decisions that he had figured it out. He thought of what Emma had said about the notions of forgiveness and how she couldn't deny that if they hadn't left Boston, she wouldn't have found the happiness she had.

He understood the meaning of that.

He would have been miserable in his own life and yet, wouldn't have even known it.

He glanced at Lillian, watching the way the darkening sky and the setting sun played along the dark strands of her hair, making them shine with a slight blue tint. He hadn't noticed her cheeks or the cute way her nose and mouth fit her face. Not only was she a lovely woman, just as Emma said, but she intrigued him more and more every day.

"Would you like to see the cattle sometime? Maybe even get on a horse and help with them?" His heart thumped with his question. He hadn't planned on asking it, but the sight of her walking along with him . . . well, he just had to ask her.

She looked over at him as her eyes widened, and she blinked. She seemed to take a gulp of breath before she finally opened her mouth. "Oh. Um, well, I . . . I don't know how to ride a horse."

He stopped walking and inhaled a deep breath. He knew he wanted to ask her a question, but he wasn't sure what her answer would be, and part of him feared the thought of what she could say. "Do . . . do you want to learn?"

She stopped walking too and faced him. Her gaze dropped to the ground, and she then looked back at him. She smiled, biting her lip for a moment before she nodded. "I do . . . or, I mean, I would like to. I've always loved horses, and I know women . . . well, women don't ride much, if at all. But it would be fun."

"All right, then. Tomorrow morning you will have your first lesson."

NINE

LILLIAN

"You are doing what?" Lillian's mother gaped at her for a moment before she folded her arms across her chest.

"I'm going to learn to ride a horse."

"But why?"

"Because I want to. Everett asked if he could teach me, and if I learned, we could watch the cattle."

Her mother's eyebrows furrowed, and she inhaled a deep breath. "But it's not . . . "

"It's not what?"

"What about your condition? I don't think you should ride a horse while carrying a child."

Lillian knew those were the words her mother was going to say before she even said them. They had been ones she'd used herself this morning as she laid under the blankets, looking up at the stars. A mix of emotions had washed through her in the hours since Everett had invited her to ride, and although she didn't know what to make of some of them, she couldn't deny that a few of them scared her.

Of course, when she learned of the baby, she was happy as

any woman would be. The chance of becoming a mother, raising a child, having someone to love, and doing right by the soul that God had blessed her with . . . what could be more of a happy moment than that?

She wanted to feel nothing but the happiness she knew she should feel.

Yet even knowing that there was a darkness to her thoughts at times.

And they were the ones that scared her.

While this baby was a blessing and a gift from her late husband—part him and part her, it was also a hindrance. Something that could make the one man she was starting to care for stop caring for her. Something that could make him leave and never speak to her again.

She didn't like thinking such things, yet she couldn't help it.

That was the reality of her situation.

That was the reality of her life.

"Well, I don't think it's anything to be concerned about." She moved around her mother, trying to pass, but before she could get more than a few steps, her mother reached out and stopped her.

"And what if something happens?"

"What is going to happen?"

"What if you fall off? You've already fallen out of the wagon. You don't need another injury. It's too much of a risk."

"But I fell out of the wagon and was all right . . ." She glanced down at her stomach, laying her hand on the tiny bump she had noticed but only because she knew what her stomach looked like. "There is nothing you can say that will stop me, Mother. I want to spend time with Everett. Besides, isn't that what you wanted? You wanted us to spend time together."

"I did. But I didn't want you to put your unborn child at risk to do it."

Lillian closed her eyes for a moment before she opened

them. "If you saw him last night when he asked me if I wanted to learn, you wouldn't be telling me no." Tears built in her eyes as she thought of their walk from the river. It was only a moment, but it was a moment where she forgot all her troubles. She wanted more of it, and for the first time, she could admit it to herself, she wanted more of Everett's company. "I'm sorry, Mother, but it's my choice."

She spun and walked away from the wagon, praying that her mother would not be so cross with her that she would follow her.

Her mother didn't.

~

By the time she'd reached the cattle herd, Lillian had worked herself into a lather. Repeating the conversation over and over in her mind, the more she thought about what she was doing and thinking, the more she felt as though she was throwing caution to the wind.

And she was never one to do that before.

She never liked to live life not knowing what the day would bring. Nor did she like anything that was a risk in her eyes. She never did anything to get herself into trouble and never put herself in harm's way. Her days were always planned—a routine that Jacob often mocked her for as being boring.

Of course, he wasn't mocking her to be mean. "It's one of the qualities I love about you the most," he often told her.

"Good morning," Everett said, tipping his hat as she approached the horses. "Are you ready to learn how to ride?"

"This is safe, right?" she asked, biting her lip.

He smiled and nodded. "Of course, it is. This is Big Brown, or at least that's what I call him." He patted the brown horse on its neck. "He's lazy and won't do anything other than walk, which is why he's on the back team and not a lead horse or a riding horse."

She glanced at him, giving him a half-smile before following him to the horse, where he showed her all the parts of the bridle and saddle, and then demonstrated how to get on and off the animal.

"Seems easy enough, right?" he asked.

"Yes." Although she wasn't lying fully, it did seem easy, it was also a lot to remember, and she didn't want to admit to herself how much her mind was reeling over all the instructions, let alone him. "I think I can manage."

"Well, all right, then." He handed her the reins. "Climb on, and we will ride to the creek and back. I figure that would be a good bit for your first time."

She smiled and nodded, taking the reins. Her heart thumped as he handed them over and made his way to his horse, climbing on as she inhaled a deep breath and stuck her foot in the stirrup. After a few bounces on her other foot, she hoisted herself into the saddle, silently praying that she would have nothing to fear, and that God would keep her safe.

"Are you ready?" Everett asked.

"I think so."

"Well, let's go."

As Everett's horse walked forward, Big Brown did too, moving underneath her. She grabbed the horn, gripping it tight. Her whole body went rigid, and her heart thumped. She didn't know what she was doing, but as the horse took several more steps, panic bubbled in her chest.

I can't do this, she thought to herself. *I shouldn't do this.*

More panic washed through her. She didn't want to get hurt, and she didn't want to hurt the baby. No matter what her feelings were or her thoughts.

She pulled the horse to a stop.

Noticing she'd stopped, Everett stopped his horse too. "Is something the matter?"

"I shouldn't do this."

"Why not?"

She glanced at him, then dropped her gaze to the ground, shaking her head. "I . . . I can't tell you why."

She knew how her words sounded, knew that they would only stir more questions into his mind—questions that he would surely ask and want answers to. She couldn't give him the answers, though, not without telling him the truth, and she couldn't bring herself to do it. Not now. Not yet.

She swung her leg over the saddle, climbing down from the horse, and as she moved toward Everett to hand him the reins, someone called her name.

"Lillian! Lillian!"

She spun to see Emma and Abby running toward her.

"Lillian!" Emma called out again.

The two stopped and waved at her. "We need your help!"

Lillian glanced at Everett as he climbed down from the horse and took the reins from her. She didn't utter a word but handed him the strips of leather and ran toward her friends.

"What is the matter?" she asked.

"It's Mrs. Baker," Emma said. She bent down, trying to catch her breath.

"She's in labor, and Sadie needs help." Abby wasn't panting as bad, but the two girls took a moment before they reached for Lillian and dragged her back to the wagons. Although she wanted to look over her shoulder at the man she had just left standing in the middle of the prairie, she didn't.

∽

*B*y the time the three women reached the campsite, Sadie had already laid out blankets and pillows and helped Mrs. Baker get comfortable in the back of the wagon.

Or at least as comfortable as she could get, Lillian guessed.

Looking at the woman and watching her heavy breathing and pained expression, Lillian wasn't sure comfort was something the woman could obtain at the moment.

"What do you need us to do?" Emma asked.

"I need you to find me a clean knife and a blanket and then clean some rags and soak them in a bucket of clean water." Although Emma's voice had cracked with worry, Sadie's was calm and to the point. She was in a doctor's frame of mind, which made Lillian long for her to be around when she went into labor.

Went into labor.

Lillian repeated the words in her head, and the more times she did, the more anxiousness rose through her body, inching across her skin and making her itch. She'd never witnessed a baby being born, and while she never thought it odd or feared having to watch it, knowing she would soon go through it . . .

It was just a thought that hadn't crossed her mind.

I'm such a fool, she thought. Here I'm worried over a man when I need to think about the baby and the fact that I will be a mother. And soon.

She cradled her forehead in her hand, closing her eyes.

"Are you all right?" a hand laid on her shoulder, and she opened her eyes to find Abby standing next to her.

"Oh. Yes. I'm just wondering what I should help with."

"Charlotte is getting the knife while Emma is getting the blanket, the rags, and the bucket of water. Sadie wants all the women to stay here and wait in case she needs something." Abby pointed to the fire. "I was thinking of making a kettle of tea. Do you want to help me?"

"Sure."

The minutes turned into hours as the women around the camp sat around, drank tea, and helped Sadie when she needed. Mrs. Baker's moans drifted into louder and louder screams, and with each one, not only would all the women cringe, but the men would too. More and more of them left the camp, leaving Mr. Baker alone with all the women, and he paced around the campfire with his eyebrows furrowed in worry.

Lillian watched the faithful husband, and with each time he would pace, spin, and pace again, her stomach twisted. She didn't want to imagine Jacob in the same situation, yet that was all she pictured—him pacing with worry and yet excited at becoming a father.

While they had talked about starting a family, it was still a what-if type of conversation, never this *for sure* thing they saw happening in months instead of years. Whether it was a name he thought of, or a blanket he would see, or even when they were walking through town and he would see a family, a pregnant woman, or one holding a baby he would point them out.

"You are going to be a wonderful mother," he would always say to her with a beaming smile and a glint in his eye.

Now, here she was, on that road, only he wouldn't be around to see it.

He also wouldn't be around to see, love, or raise their child.

His child.

His son or daughter.

Mrs. Baker let out several more screams before there was a moment of silence followed by the cries of an infant. Mr. Baker exhaled a deep breath, and as he rushed toward the wagon, Sadie climbed down and moved to him with a wrapped bundle in her arms.

"It's a boy," she said.

"I have a son?" With his arms outstretched, he froze, and as she nodded, he melted, taking the infant from her and cradling it in his arms. "I have a son. You shall be called Arthur Matthew after your mother's father and grandfather."

Sadie smiled. "That sounds like the perfect name for a boy who will grow up into a strong man."

Mr. Baker beamed as he stared down at his son. All the women surrounded him, and as he moved around in circles, they gushed; a few even reached out, stroking the infant on his head while they *ooohed* and *aahed* over him.

"He's beautiful," they all said, and after a few more gushed about the baby, Mr. Baker made his way to the wagon to take the boy back to his mother, giving all the women one last wave as though he was giving them a silent thank you for their help.

They all waved back.

"Isn't it wonderful?" Emma asked. "I can't believe we just witnessed that. There is another person in the world. Can you believe it?"

"I can't believe how tiny he is." Abby hooked her arm through Emma's and rested her head on Emma's shoulder. She heaved a deep sigh before letting out a soft giggle. "It makes me want to start a family."

Emma chuckled. "I must say it makes me want to start one too."

Lillian snorted with their confession. "I already have."

The words left her lips before she could stop them, and as Emma and Abby gasped and stared at her, she slapped her hand over her mouth.

What had she just done?

TEN

LILLIAN

There had been very few times in Lillian's life that she wished she could be in another place. Once when she was ten years old, another girl in her school class had dumped a box of mud and frogs on her desk, and as she screamed and tried to run, she tripped and fell, landing on her face on the schoolhouse floor. Everyone laughed and pointed, and she could remember all she wanted was to go home.

This was and yet wasn't like that time.

It was in that she wanted to go home—or at least to the wagon. And it wasn't in that right now; she would rather deal with a box full of mud and frogs than deal with the fact that she'd just told Emma and Abby the truth about her without even meaning to.

"I'm sorry, but what did you say?" Emma asked.

"I didn't say anything."

"No. You did. You said you already started one. One what? A family? What are you talking about?"

Lillian's blood ran cold, and her knees weakened. She could try to lie and talk herself out of it, back peddling somehow while she hoped and prayed they would go along with it. Or she could just tell them the truth about everything.

She heaved a deep sigh, letting her shoulders hunch with her shame.

"I've . . . I've been keeping a secret from you," she finally said.

While Abby's brow furrowed, Emma folded her arms across her chest. "And what secret is that?" the latter asked.

Lillian dropped her gaze to the ground, studying the thin and thick blades of tall prairie grass.

"Well . . . I'm a widow. I was married, and my husband died."

"What did he die from?"

"An accident at the sawmill he worked for. He was crushed when several logs broke free and rolled down the hill. Several men died, actually."

Abby covered her mouth with her hand. Her eyes widened, then misted with tears. "I'm so sorry."

Emma said nothing but continued to stare at Lillian with one eyebrow raised. She inhaled and exhaled several deep breaths as though they helped her better process what Lillian was saying.

"And so . . ." Abby said, looking down at Lillian's stomach. "You're carrying his child."

Lillian nodded. "I found out after we left Missouri."

"So, you've known the whole time?" Emma asked.

"Not the whole time. It was a couple of weeks after we left." Lillian paused as she tried to fight off the regret and shame. "We were married when I conceived. I haven't disgraced my family with any scandal."

Abby shook her head. "We didn't think it was." She glanced at Emma, who still hadn't said a word. "Well, at least I don't think that." She nudged Emma with her shoulder. "Emma? Are you going to say anything?"

Emma swallowed as though a lump had formed in her

throat. She blinked as she took another couple of deep breaths, and she lifted her hand, laying it on her collarbone.

"I . . . I don't know what to say," she finally said.

"I understand." Lillian's heart thumped, and she dropped her gaze to the ground once more.

"But I do have one question," Emma continued.

"What is that?"

"Have you told my brother the truth? Or have you kept it from him?"

Lillian closed her eyes. Her stomach clenched, and for the first time, it wasn't just in the morning time that she felt sick to her stomach.

~

EVERETT

*E*verett had watched Lillian as she fled toward camp with Emma and Abby. Although he knew they had called her because she was needed in camp, he also felt that even if they hadn't come, she would have left anyway. Something had triggered her and caused her to panic, and while he didn't want to believe it was him, the concern was still there.

Had he done something wrong? Said something wrong? Had he been too forward? He didn't know how he had been. He hadn't said anything to her that concerned him or that he stopped and thought it wrong.

He climbed down from his horse, tying Big Brown to the tree before making his way over to the cowboy's camp and grabbing a scoopful of water.

"How's it going?" he asked Willy and Beau.

They both looked up from their supper and shrugged. "We'll see when we head back there in a bit. Just needed to fill our stomachs," Willy said, motioning toward some of the herd.

Although they weren't close, the men could still see them just in case. "Mr. Garrison and Mr. Campbell are out there now. They will head into camp come supper time."

"I think I'll head out and check to see how they are."

Before Willy could say another word, Everett climbed back on his horse and galloped for the cattle, finding James and William standing near the river under the shade of a tree.

"How are you doing today, gentlemen?" he asked.

William yawned. "I can't believe you talked me into this watch schedule. This is the most boring job I've ever had in my entire life."

"This is nothing compared to a night watch in the cavalry." James removed his hat with one hand while he yanked a handkerchief and dabbed his forehead with the other. "At least there are others around to talk to. I used to have to scout around the fort all by myself."

The three men exchanged glances, and James heaved a deep sigh. "I don't miss those days."

"I don't think I would either." William adjusted his hat and then cleared his throat, coughing a few times as though he wanted to clear out his pipes.

"So," James looked at Everett, "How did the riding lesson go?" A broad grin spread across Everett's brother-in-law's face, and he winked.

"Honestly, not well."

"Why? What happened?"

"We rode all of a few minutes before she said she shouldn't learn and climbed down off the horse and started walking back to camp. Then my sister and Abby came to get her because they needed her help with Mrs. Baker."

"Did she say why she shouldn't ride?"

Everett shook his head. "Not a word. I don't know what happened."

"So, if my wife hadn't come for her, do you think you could

have stopped her?" James' horse adjusted its weight, cocking one leg, and James leaned in the other direction to counter his balance.

"I don't know." Everett shrugged. "She seemed quite determined to get away from the horse and me."

"I wonder what happened."

The three men exchanged glances again, and while James' brow furrowed in confusion, Willian rubbed his chin as though doing so helped him think. It didn't seem to work, for he had no advice to give. In fact, he didn't say anything at all.

"What are you going to do?" James asked.

"I don't know. I suppose I can speak to her about it. But I don't wish to make her feel uncomfortable."

"No, you certainly don't want to do that. Still, she should at least allow you to ask her some questions and get some answers."

"I suppose I could just let it go and not say anything. I was only trying to teach her to ride. It wasn't like I intended to propose or anything like that."

"Are you sure about that?" James cocked his head to the side, raising one eyebrow.

"You just take your thoughts and shove them where the sun doesn't shine." A slight chuckle whispered through Everett's chest, and although he thought there was a hint of amusement in what he said, he couldn't deny that there was also a twinge of disappointment. In truth, he hadn't thought of proposing. Not in the slightest. But it would have been nice to spend time with Lillian. His feelings for her had grown so much, and they continued to every day. He didn't want to admit that he could see her as his wife. But he also couldn't deny it either.

"Why don't you ask her if she wants to try again?" William asked.

"I suppose I could."

"Mr. Russell told Abby and me about the cliffs about half a mile from here. People have carved their names in the rock."

"What for?"

"To show they were there. Perhaps you could take her there and let her carve her name in the rock too."

"And what would that do?"

William shrugged. "I suppose nothing. It's just something fun. Abby enjoyed it. It made her feel as though no matter what happened to us, whether we lived five more years, ten more years, or to a ripe old age, we will always be here in this place . . . sort of at least. People will pass the mountain, read our names, and know we were here."

"That sounds nice and interesting too."

"We thought so."

The more Everett thought about taking her out to the cliffs, the more excited he felt, and although there was a little apprehension in his stomach as he didn't know if she would agree to come with him, he hoped that if he told her what he planned for them, she might be more inclined to say yes.

Or at least he hoped that would be the case.

"I think I'll ride back to the wagons and ask her."

James pointed over Everett's shoulder. "I don't think you will have to ride that far."

"Why not?"

"Because she's right over there."

Everett spun his horse around, catching sight of Lillian standing several dozen yards from them. Her hands were clasped at her waist, but she waved as she noticed him see her. A slight smile inched through half of her lips.

"I'll see you later, gentlemen," he said to the men, cueing his horse into a trot as he made his way toward her.

ELEVEN

LILLIAN

*L*illian's heart thumped as Everett rode toward her. Although she'd thought of what she would say—even practicing it a few times as she walked out to the herd —seeing him making his way toward her caused her to forget every word she'd even thought of.

"They told me I could find you here." She hooked her thumb over toward the cowboy's camp.

"I was checking on things one last time before heading back to the wagons."

"Is everything all right?" She knew her question was nothing more than casual, meaningless banter, but she couldn't help herself. She needed more time, more distractions. Although she knew she needed to get to the point, she wasn't ready.

Even if she should be.

"Seems to be. They should be fine for the night."

"That's good."

She tried to smile, but it felt awkward and forced, and they stared at each other for a moment without saying a word.

"How is Mrs. Baker?" he finally asked.

"She's good. It was a boy. They have a son."

"That's wonderful."

"He's tiny. Tinier than I thought he would be. I don't know why. I guess it's been a long time since I've seen a newborn." She paused, thinking of the last time. She couldn't place it. "Actually, I don't think I've ever seen a baby right after it was born. I have cousins, but they were always a few months to a year old before I saw them."

"I've never seen a newborn either, so I'll have to take your word for it."

Silence fell over them both again, but instead of staring at each other, Lillian dropped her gaze to the floor. While one voice inside her head told her to explain what had happened, another screamed that she wasn't ready.

He cleared his throat. "Do you . . . do you think we could try that ride again? William was telling me about a place he took Abby and . . . well, it sounds rather interesting. I thought perhaps you would want to see it."

"Where is it?"

"He said about a half of a mile from here. It's not far. We won't be gone long and should be back well before supper."

She inhaled a deep breath, exhaling slowly. She knew this was the chance, the moment she would have to take in order to tell him the truth. It was what he deserved, after all. Not to mention, Emma told her that if she didn't tell him tonight, Emma would.

"All right."

She followed him back to the cowboy's camp, inhaling another deep breath as she climbed into the saddle and cued Big Brown to follow Everett's horse. They rode through the tall grass, and although she feared the risk she took, the more Big Brown moved quietly underneath her, the more she felt at ease. He really was nothing more than a gentle giant.

They continued riding through the meadow until they came upon the trail that curved through a ravine, surrounding them with tall cliffs. Everett pulled his horse to a stop, and as he dismounted, Lillian stopped too. She swung her leg over, climbing down with a little less grace than him. As her feet hit the ground, her weight knocked her off balance, and her knees nearly buckled. Everett reached out, grabbing her before she fell, and with his arms wrapped around her, their gazes locked.

She sucked in a breath.

"I'm sorry," he said, releasing her. "I just didn't want you to fall."

"It's all right. I wouldn't have wanted to fall." She chuckled, cocking her head to the side in the hope that the hint of mirth would help ease the awkwardness of the moment. It did.

"So, where are we?" she asked.

"William said that Mr. Russell told him that people carve their names into the rocks of the cliffs. He said it's called Register Cliffs or something like that. I thought maybe you would like to carve your name."

"Is there a reason to do it?"

"He said it was just something that shows we were here. Who knows how long the carved names will be around. For all we know, people living a hundred years from now might pass through here and read all the names. Wouldn't it be special to have them read your name?"

A tiny flicker of curiosity and excitement bubbled in her chest. She didn't know if it was the thought of someone reading her name long after she's gone that piqued her interest or the way his tone drew her in with his own excitement that made her want to do it.

"That sounds like fun."

"Yeah? I think so too." He turned to his saddle and dug through the saddlebags, yanking out a large knife. "Let's go."

Leaving the horses to graze on the grass around the cliffs, she followed him to the side of the mountain. Names popped out from the rock the closer they got to the mountain, and she reached out, tracing her fingers over some of them.

"John Malcolm," she said, reading one of them. "1840. That was fifteen years ago."

"I wonder if he's still alive and where he's living."

"Me too."

They glanced at each other, chuckling.

"Is it odd to wonder about a stranger?" he asked her.

"I don't think so. But if it is, I suppose we can be odd together."

They continued reading over the names, reading most of them aloud. While most had the name and year, some had the name and age of the person, and she took a little longer to read the names of a family of six that had passed through just a few short years ago. The youngest of their family was a year old, while the oldest child was thirteen.

She wondered how the children were doing now. Was the oldest starting a new life of his own? Had he and his brothers and sister survived? Or had they succumbed to the harshness of the trail or frontier? She thought about the people who could read her name in five or ten years. Would they wonder the same about her?

Surely, they would just as she did to those who came before her.

"Are you ready?" Everett held the knife in his hand, outstretching it for her to take. Her heart thumped as she grabbed it from him.

"Where should I carve it?" she asked.

His brow furrowed, and he glanced around the side of the mountain, walking a few feet away from her as he hemmed and hawed over a few different spots.

"What about right here?" he asked, finally stopping and pointing to a spot at the perfect height for her.

"All right." She moved over to the spot, biting her lip as she began scratching the blade against the rock. "Should I just put my name and the year?"

"Put whatever you want."

She continued to carve through all the letters of her name, finishing with the year, before handing the knife to him. He took it from her, smiling.

"Do you mind if I carve my name next to yours?"

"Not at all."

As he took the knife to the rock, she glanced around, bending down to touch a few flowers blooming through the tufts of the grass. Their white petals fluttered in the slight breeze, and although she could still feel the weight of knowing what she had to do, they made her smile. Surely, they were nothing more than weeds yet, they were still beautiful in their own right.

Perhaps they were like her.

Or she was like them.

Just weeds—or a tarnished soul—there was still beauty in them.

Was that what this child would bring? Beauty in all the ashes of her forever changed life? While she would live in fear of another man rejecting her, she would also live in love. Love for another being that was of her flesh and blood.

What was wrong with that?

Nothing.

There was nothing wrong with that.

"Well. I think I'm done. What do you think?" Everett backed away from the rock, and as Lillian straightened back up, she looked at their names.

Everett Ford, 1855 loves Lillian Jones, 1855

Her heart thumped, and her breath quickened. She took a few steps back, dropping her gaze to the ground. He reached out, grabbing her hand.

"Lillian, are you all right?"

"You shouldn't . . . you shouldn't have written that."

"Why not? It's the truth." He heaved a deep sigh, looking out over the horizon before reaching for her chin and drawing her eyes to his. "I've been fighting it for who knows how long, and I don't want to fight it anymore. So often, my sister or James would say something, and I would argue with them, telling them I had no intentions for you. But it's not true. I do. Please, just . . . just tell me how you feel. Do you love me?"

It was the one question she'd wanted to hear from him for so long. Yet it was also the question she feared the most, and not because she couldn't answer it, but because she could. And it was an answer she didn't want to give.

Life forced her to say no.

Even if her heart didn't want to.

"It's not that simple." She tried to take a few more steps away from him, but he held onto her hand.

"Yes, it is."

She shook her head. "No. It's not. And there's a reason it's not. I . . . I have something to tell you."

He inhaled a sharp breath and released his grip, dropping her hand. "There is another man in Oregon, isn't there?" He looked down at the ground. His voice deepened with disappointment.

"No, there isn't another man in Oregon. But there was another man in Missouri. He was my husband, and he died. I am a widow."

"Why didn't you tell anyone?"

"I don't know. It was easier to lie." She closed her eyes and bit her lip. There was another part to the story she needed to tell him, and she was sure he wouldn't be as understanding. "There's more. I'm . . . I'm carrying his child."

Everett inhaled another sharp breath, taking a few steps away from her this time. He looked all around at the mountains around them before he cleared his throat. "I see."

"So, you can understand why I can't . . . and we can't."

He clenched his jaw, and his eyes narrowed as though he was annoyed with his own thoughts—whatever they were. "I don't care about the fact that you were married, and even though . . . another man's baby would be a hard adjustment. It wouldn't have been a reason that stopped me from loving you or wanting to be with you." He backed away a few more steps and shook his head. "You lied to me. You lied to everyone."

"I know."

"I don't know if I can accept that. I . . . I need some time."

She closed her eyes, trying to ignore the crushing blow to her heart.

He backed away even more steps. "Do . . . do you think you could make it back to the camp? I mean, I don't want to leave you . . ."

"I'll be fine. It's not far."

"Are you sure?"

"Yes." Tears mocked her, and she closed her eyes again, pinching her arm with her fingers to keep them at bay. She didn't want to cry in front of him or make him feel bad. It wasn't his fault. None of it was. He wasn't the cause of her pain. She was. She'd caused it all.

She turned back toward the rocks, staring at the words they'd just carved into the stone as she listened to him walk away, climb onto his horse, and cue it into a gallop. She wanted to go after him, begging for forgiveness, yet she couldn't.

She'd done so much wrong, and as she made her way over to Big Brown and climbed on, the only thought that came to her was to flee.

Go far away where she wouldn't hurt anyone, especially those she loved.

Instead of turning back toward the camp, she turned away from it, cueing Big Brown to go deeper into the ravine and into the mountains.

TWELVE

EVERETT

*E*verett nearly turned around several times as he rode back to camp. He wanted to go back to Lillian, yet there was also a pain in him that stopped him. He could probably see past the husband and child, although he couldn't deny those things were hard to think about. But the lying. It was all too much to take in at the moment. He needed time. He needed space.

He'd already been through the lies of his father and how they destroyed everything. Of course, he had come to know a life that was better than what he would have had, but the lies just brought up so many emotions.

He didn't know what to do.

"Where is Lillian," Emma asked as he rode up to her wagon and stopped his horse.

"She's heading back to camp. I probably shouldn't have left her alone, but she said she was all right."

"Did she tell you?"

"Yes." He hung his head, dropping his gaze to the ground. His heart hurt. "Did you know?"

"No. I didn't. She let it slip this morning after Mrs. Baker delivered her baby. I was so shocked. I didn't even see it coming."

He nodded. "She lied to us. She lied to everyone."

"I know."

"Just like Father lied to us."

"I know that too. I'm so sorry."

"I don't know what to do." He inhaled a deep breath, letting it out as he glanced up at the sky. "I know I'm asked to give grace and forgiveness."

"Yes, you are. But you are also allowed to feel hurt."

"Am I?" He snorted, shaking his head as he looked at his sister.

Her eyebrows were furrowed not in anger but of a deep concern he hadn't seen since the night of the party where their father's secrets were spilled for everyone to know. He didn't want to remember that night, yet it was all that came to his head since finding out that Lillian had lied to him.

"How do you feel about her being married and a widow?" Emma asked.

"I . . . I don't really mind that. I was never the type that . . . needed . . . it wasn't like she." He took a few breaths. "She fell in love, they were married, and he died. If that was the case for you . . . I wouldn't want a man holding that against you. It's not her fault he died. She couldn't have predicted it."

"No, she couldn't." Emma paused. "What about the baby?"

He glanced out over the camp, watching the people linger about their wagons. Some were doing chores—cooking, washing the laundry—and some were already sitting down to their supper, and he watched the families more than the rest. They looked happy. They looked peaceful. He'd always wanted to be a father. Of course, he imagined that would be years from now after he'd found a woman to love and they were married. But he still thought it would be something for them to share—their own flesh and blood made from half her and half him.

This baby wouldn't be his.

He could love it, and he would, but it wouldn't be the same.

"I don't know. I thought I always fancied myself as a man who would step up for a child and raise him or her as my own if the situation warranted it."

"But?"

"I don't know if there is a but. You know I wouldn't turn away a child. Especially one who lost a father without ever knowing the man." Everett rested his hands on his hips. "It's the lying. I just don't understand why she didn't tell anyone. Why she didn't tell you. Why she didn't tell me."

"I don't know why she didn't." He glanced up, looking over at her parents, who were moving around the wagon—his wagon —as they prepared for supper. "Do you think her parents told her not to tell anyone?"

"I don't know."

"They don't seem like dishonest people." His brow furrowed, and he growled as he spun and ran his hands through his hair. He grabbed it by the roots, yanking on it for a moment as though the distraction of pain in his scalp would somehow ease the burden of the whole mess.

Of course, it didn't work.

"How am I going to face them tonight?" He spun back around toward Emma.

"You're more than welcome to have supper with James and me. And I will fetch your things if you wish to sleep under our wagon instead of theirs."

He shook his head. No matter how much he wanted to take Emma up on her offer, he knew he couldn't. If he did, it would be running away from the problem, and that wasn't something he wanted to do. Ever. He'd run away from Boston, and although it was the best choice and he was forced to instead of by his own accord, he never wanted to do it again.

"No, you don't have to do that. I need to face this and deal with it."

He made his way to his horse, untying its reins from the wagon before grabbing his hat from the saddle horn and sliding it back onto his head.

"Mr. Ford!" a voice called out. He turned to see Mr. Russell trotting toward them, waving. "Mrs. Garrison!"

The older man panted as he approached them, bending down for a moment to catch his breath. "I'm glad I caught you."

"What seems to be the matter, Mr. Russell?" Emma asked as she looked from Everett to the wagon master. She raised one eyebrow.

"A storm is coming, and it's heading our way. I saw the clouds and . . . well, I don't think we will miss it. It's coming straight for us."

"How bad is it?" Everett asked. His stomach twisted.

"Hard to say. But the dark clouds tell me it won't be light rain. It's probably best we load up the wagons and move toward the mountains. At least there we might find some shelter."

Everett didn't know what he hated more, hearing a storm was coming or the tone of Mr. Russell's words. Although the wagon master tried to hide it, Everett heard the worry woven in his words and the concern behind his eyes.

"What about the cattle?"

"The boys are already rounding them up and taking them to the ravine." Mr. Russell hooked his thumb over his shoulder. "I told Mr. Garrison and Mr. Campbell to return to the camp, they shouldn't be long."

"That's all right. I know what I need to do." Emma glanced between the wagon master and Everett, and with a sigh on her lips, she got to work, gathering the supplies she'd laid out to start supper.

"When you're ready, just head north about a half of a mile.

You can't miss the cliffs." Mr. Russell looked at Everett. "Can you tell Mr. and Mrs. Jones?"

"Of course. And I'll head out to help with the cattle."

"Well, I don't think Willy and Beau will need it, but I can't say they won't appreciate it. The cows already seemed restless when I was out there telling them about the weather." Mr. Russell tipped his hat, not waiting around for another word from either brother or sister before he trotted off to the next wagon.

"Do you want me to tell Mr. and Mrs. Jones?" Emma asked Everett.

He shook his head. "Nah. I'll do it as I leave to go help with the cattle. Lillian should be along shortly. See that you get Big Brown secured with your horses for me. She's riding him."

"I will."

Everett led his horse away from Emma's wagon toward Mr. and Mrs. Jones while she continued gathering all her belongings and packing them back into the wagon. He didn't want to speak to Lillian's parents any more than he wanted to speak to her right now. He needed time to think about everything. He needed distance.

"Mr. Ford? I didn't know you were back. Did Lillian find you?" Mrs. Jones looked up from the pot of stew hanging over the fire as he approached. A smile beamed across her face.

"Yes. She did."

"And do you know where she is now?" Mrs. Jones glanced around him and the camp.

"I don't, actually. We were riding and . . . well, I needed to head back to camp. She should be along shortly." He inhaled a deep breath. "The reason I came by is to let you know that a storm is headed for us. Mr. Russell wants everyone to pack up their wagons and head for the mountains. We will be safer there."

"Oh." She straightened her shoulders and nodded. "All right. We will get everything packed up right now."

"I'm going to head out to help with the cattle, so I'll leave everything in your hands."

"Yes, of course. We will make sure to take good care of all the animals and see to every one of them."

"Thank you." He tipped his hat toward the woman and moved around to the side of the horse, sticking his foot in the stirrup before climbing in the saddle. He cued the horse to walk, but as it took the first few steps, Mrs. Jones rushed toward him, waving her arm.

"She told you. Didn't she?"

He glanced at the woman and then at the ground. "Yes, she did."

"She hated not telling you. She wanted to, but she didn't want to hurt you."

Everett glanced down at Mrs. Jones for a moment before he looked out upon the horizon. This is why he didn't want to talk to the woman. He knew she would know, and he knew she would try to reason with him. Not that he thought she shouldn't. It was her daughter. She had every right to come to her defense or aid. But it didn't mean he was ready to hear what she had to say.

Without meeting her gaze, he continued to stare off in the distance. "Thank you for packing up the wagon. I best be getting to the cattle to make sure they are all right."

"Of course." She backed away, her shoulders hunched.

He hated his rudeness, but he rode away without another word.

~

*B*y the time he found Willy and Beau, the cowboys had already started herding the cattle toward the mountains. Sensing the rain and hearing the thunder, the cattle had grown anxious, and as the wind blew in, they startled easier. While most of them stayed together, not wishing to leave their herd mates, a few would dart off in different directions, confused and scared by the blowing trees, cracks of lightning, or roll of thunder.

Everett chased down each cow that tried to get away, driving them back to the herd as they pushed them farther and farther into the depths of the mountains and down into a pocket-like meadow.

"They should be fine here," Willy said, shouting over the loud storm moving around them. He pointed back down the trail. "We should get to the wagons and see if anyone needs help."

"Are you sure no one should stay with the herd?" Everett asked.

Beau shook his head. "You can if you want, but they should stay here. If they are dumb enough to leave, they deserve what they get."

Everett grimaced. Although he knew that it was foolish to risk his life for any of the cattle, it was also his—and everyone else's—food Beau was talking about, including his own. Losing even just one cow could mean them going weeks without food. He couldn't let that happen.

"I think I'll stay here," he said.

Both Willy and Beau shrugged.

"Suit yourself," Willy said.

The two rode off while Everett climbed down from the horse and led him down into a thicket. The wind ripped through the branches and leaves, and Everett crouched in the thick of them, wiggling his hat farther down around his ears.

His horse moved in close, sticking his butt toward the wind; its tail blew in all directions.

Lightning cracked above his head, and with the roar of the thunder, rain poured down upon him. His horse pinned its ears and moved closer into the thicket. He glanced around at the cows who moved into the nearest bushes around them. Part of him regretted not leaving and heading back to the wagons, yet the other part of him wanted to be as far away from other people as he could get. He needed time to himself to think about Lillian and what happened between them.

THIRTEEN

LILLIAN

The wind swirled around Lillian, and Big Brown lifted his head. His ears perked, moving forward and backward while he took several deep breaths as though he caught the scent of something. Lillian looked up, gasping at the sight of the dark clouds. She'd never seen that deep color of blue in them before, and as she watched the storm roll in, a flash of lightning cracked, and thunder boomed.

Big Brown lifted his head higher and made a long vibrating snort sound. His body tightened underneath her, and he pranced a few steps.

"Whoa," she said, pulling back on the reins. "Easy. It's just the storm." She glanced up again as the wind kicked up more. "A storm I think we should get out of."

She glanced around, finding a crevice in the side of the mountain. It wouldn't be the best cover, but it would be better than staying out on the open trail. She swung her leg over, climbing down from the saddle before throwing the reins over Big Brown's head and leading him off the trail. Although he followed her, his head was high, and he snorted and danced as she led him along.

"It's all right," she told him, trying to stroke his face and nose.

He didn't listen.

Or perhaps she didn't calm him enough.

She reached up to touch his nose again, and he jumped, bolting a few steps before he hit the end of the slack in the reins.

"Whoa! Whoa! Easy." Although he stopped and didn't try to run again, he chewed on the bit. His breathing deepened, and she could see the whites of his eyes. She hurried toward the bushes and rocks and crouched down, hiding in the branches and leaves. It wasn't big enough to accommodate them both, at least not fully, but she tugged on the reins, trying to get him in as much as she could.

Another flash of lightning cracked, and thunder rumbled. Rain poured down, drenching her and Big Brown within seconds.

She thought of her parents and of Everett, and she hoped and prayed they were safe, even if she didn't know if she was. She also prayed that they would understand why she left, that they would see the reasons as she saw them.

It's just better this way, she thought. Better that I leave and never return. Better that they can have lives without care or concern for what happened to her. It was her fault they were out in the storm and her fault they sold everything they owned, trekking out to the dangerous frontier. And her fault they left everything they'd ever known behind. They should be in their warm home, the one they lived in since she was an infant. The one they thought they would live in forever.

"It's my fault they aren't." Although she knew no one was around, she spoke as though someone was listening. She spoke to God. "Keep them safe. Let them be happy in this new life when I have destroyed their old one. Let them understand I didn't mean to ruin everything, even if I did. And, God, please find a way to tell Everett I'm sorry. I shouldn't have lied. All I've done . . . is told lies. To everyone."

I don't deserve this, she thought. I don't deserve any of this.

She jumped to her feet and threw the reins over Big Brown's neck. If he wanted to leave, he was more than welcome. Hopefully, he would find the wagon train, or one of the men on the wagon train would find him. With a final pat on his nose, she moved around him, darting out from the protection of the bushes, and headed out into the middle of the trail. Rain poured from the sky, blinding her as she looked up at the darkness.

"You can take me," she shouted. "Just take me. Please just take me."

~

EVERETT

*D*renched and frozen, Everett shivered as he climbed back onto his horse. He didn't know how he'd lived through the storm, and part of him didn't think he would want to know the answer.

Sheer luck came to mind. That, or just the fact that God wanted to throw a lifeline to someone stupid enough to try to ride out a storm while crouched in a thicket of bushes.

"It's probably the latter," he said to himself as he cued the horse down the trail.

He found the wagons not far from where he and the cattle rode out the storm, and while everyone looked as wet and worn as he felt, the damage seemed minimal. Only one wagon was missing its bonnet, and another was missing a horse.

"It ran off after a bolt of lightning hit the side of the mountain. We can try to find it, but at this point, I'd say looking for it would be just a waste of time," Mr. Russell said to Mr. and Mrs.

Baker as Everett rode up. "Mr. Ford." The wagon master tipped his hat and continued to tell the husband and wife they would be more than fine with three horses instead of four.

"They are more than welcome to one of mine," he said. "I have two horses that could use the work since Mr. and Mrs. Jones took over my wagon."

While Mr. Baker smiled and moved toward him to shake his hand, Mrs. Baker's eyes filled with tears, and she clutched her newborn son tight in her arms.

"Bless you," she said.

Looking at the woman and infant, a twist of guilt prickled in his chest, and he gave them a nod before cueing his horse to continue on, and telling Mr. Baker to come by the wagon at any time to get the horse.

"Aren't you a sight for sore eyes?" Emma crouched near her wagon, and she stood as Everett rode toward her. James jumped down from the back of the wagon, carrying a sack of flour in his arms. He threw it on the ground and waved.

"It's good to see you made it through the storm," Everett said to his sister and brother-in-law.

"It's good to see you did too." Emma glanced at her husband. "Is it ruined?"

"Most of it. We can dump what is, though, and keep the rest." James yanked his knife from his pocket and cut open the bag, dumping out the flour that seemed to have gotten wet in the rain. It fell out in chunks, breaking open as it hit the ground.

"Save what you can. We can make the rest last if we have to." Emma turned back to her brother. "So, where were you?"

"I stayed with the cattle. Found shelter in some bushes."

"Are you hungry?"

"A bit. I need to do something first, though."

She nodded, glancing down at the ground for a moment before looking up at him as though she knew what that something was. Perhaps she did. She wasn't a foolish woman by any means. She also knew Everett better than he knew himself—or at least sometimes he thought she did.

"I wish I had advice for you," she said.

He slightly snorted. "I wish you did too."

Without another word, he squeezed his horse and moved past Emma's wagon, heading down the line toward the wagon he once called his own. He'd thought about what he was going to say to Lillian throughout most of the night and as he left the cattle this morning. No matter how many times he repeated the words in his head, though, they often sounded wrong.

The problem was, he didn't know if they would ever sound right.

Mr. and Mrs. Jones were moving around the wagon, checking supplies and cleaning up just as everyone else, and Mrs. Jones smiled as he approached.

"Mr. Ford?" she said, nodding to him. "Good to see you made it."

"Good to see you did too."

She glanced around him. "Where is Lillian?"

His stomach twisted. "I was just about to ask you the same thing."

"She isn't with you?" Mrs. Jones's once huge smile vanished in a sea of worry that etched through her face. Her tone deepened.

"She was supposed to return to the camp."

"She never did. We thought perhaps she met up with you and went with you to check on the cattle."

His stomach twisted even more, and his breath quickened. "I haven't seen her."

Mrs. Jones bit her lip and then screamed for her husband. The panic in the whites of her eyes sent a chill through him, and he wasted no time, not even telling them he would find her before he jerked the horse to turn around and kicked it into a gallop.

He didn't know if she was on the prairie or in the mountains, but he would start with the mountains, and he wouldn't stop searching until he found her, even if it took every moment of the rest of his life.

FOURTEEN

LILLIAN

*S*omething brushed up against Lillian's arm, and she jerked awake. Big Brown stood over her, and he nudged her again with his nose before he moved onto a patch of grass, ripping off the tall blades and chewing on it.

She sat up, glancing around at the cliffs and the sky. The storm had passed, and the sun was shining. Both she and Big Brown were still wet, and while he had started to dry in places, her hair and dress were still soaked through the bone. She rose to her feet, brushing the dirt and twigs from her dress as best she could. Her wet skirt stuck to her legs, and the material tugged tight against her. Ice cold, it made her shiver even more.

Her stomach growled, and her mouth was parched. She needed food and water, and while she knew she could find a river to solve one of her problems, the only solution to the other one was trying to find the wagons.

And that wasn't something she wanted to do.

Why didn't He take me in the storm, she thought.

She moved around to the stirrup, and as she lifted her leg, Big Brown raised his head. His ears perked. Lillian glanced over her shoulder, squinting as she looked around the landscape.

"What is it?" she asked the horse. "What do you see?"

Her heart thumped. For a moment, she imagined Everett riding down the trail. She didn't want him to find her. She didn't want anyone to find her.

Big Brown lifted his head higher, and he breathed heavier as though he caught the scent of something. He snorted and backed up several steps. Lillian clutched onto the reins. The image of Everett approaching vanished, and now she feared it was something else.

Something neither her nor Big Brown was going to like.

As if it read her mind, a mountain lion jumped out of some bushes up the trail. It stopped and stared at the horse and Lillian, and while she sucked in a breath, Big Brown danced around.

"No. No. Don't do that. Just stay still," she whispered. "Moving will only attract it."

Her heart pounded. She had to get in the saddle. But she didn't know how safe she would be. Yes, she'd be able to outrun the big cat, but she'd never galloped on a horse before.

If she fell off . . .

Standing here wasn't a choice either. She knew she couldn't run fast enough to escape.

The cat pinned its ears and hissed, trotting a few steps toward them and then stopping. Big Brown snorted again and backed up too, throwing his head. Lillian gripped the reins, moving with the horse.

She had no other choice. She'd have to ride out of here.

She darted toward the stirrup, lifting her leg. Big Brown moved from underneath her, throwing his head again. The reins jerked in her hands, and her fingers slipped on the leather. The mountain lion trotted toward them again, hissing and swiping at them with his massive paws. Big Brown whinnied and reared, knocking Lillian to the ground. Her rump hit the dirt, and the horse yanked the reins from her grasp. Big Brown jumped to the side as the cat lunged for the horse, swiping Big Brown's shoulder with his paw. Lillian screamed as the horse spun and ran off down the trail.

Lillian scrambled to her feet, watching the two run away from her. She didn't want anything to happen to Big Brown, but if the cat chased the horse, she might have a chance.

The big cat followed for several yards before it seemed to give up and stop.

Lillian sucked in a breath as it turned around and looked straight at her.

~

EVERETT

*E*verett galloped along the trail, stopping only to check for tracks or any other sign of Lillian and Big Brown. The rain had washed away any hoofprints, and the more he searched and found nothing, the more annoyance bubbled in his chest.

He never meant to upset her so much that she would run away. He just needed time to think. He wished he could go back in time and do and say things differently. Perhaps she wouldn't have run off.

He didn't know if he could ever forgive himself for what he'd done, and all he knew was that when he found her—he wasn't about to say if he found her—but when he found her, he wouldn't let even an hour go by without her in his life. Widow or not. Child or not. He would marry her and raise that baby as his own, loving them both for the rest of the days that God would bless him with on this earth.

A woman's scream echoed through the canyon.

His heart thumped, and his breathing quickened.

He spurred his horse back into a gallop, weaving down the

trail through the rocks and bushes. As his horse jumped over a fallen log, Big Brown rushed past him, galloping in the other direction.

Lillian screamed again, and Everett pushed his horse to an even faster pace.

He couldn't let anything happen to her.

He wouldn't let anything happen to her.

~

LILLIAN

*A*s the mountain lion turned and faced her, Lillian sucked in a breath.

Stay or flee? Stay or flee?

If she stayed, she could scare off the beast. But if she fled . . .

I can't outrun it, she thought. *I know I can't.*

She backed away from the big cat, taking one step at a time. It advanced, sometimes only taking a few steps and sometimes lunging for her with its ears pinned. It hissed and growled.

She backed up a few more steps, glancing around the ground for anything she could use. A rock. A stick. Anything. She found a few rocks, and she bent down, grabbing them. Her movement caused the cat to lunge again and swipe at her, hissing.

She threw the rock, missing the cat by at least a foot. It jumped, turning toward where the rock landed before turning back to her. She threw a few more rocks. Each one missed the cat, and instead of making it run away, it only seemed to anger the animal more.

She continued walking backward, noticing a tree mere feet from her. She knew cats could climb, but perhaps if she could get high enough . . . maybe it would lose interest . . .

It was a chance and a risky one at that, but it was all she could think of.

She bent down, grabbing a few more rocks and throwing them as quick as she could, distracting the mountain lion as she rushed for the tree and climbed up the trunk.

Her nails dug into the bark, filling with dirt and chunks that sliced her fingertips. She heard the cat growl and hiss, and as she scaled the trunk, she glimpsed flashes of light brown running around the tree.

The cat circled her and then jumped.

She closed her eyes, bracing for its teeth and claws.

A gunshot echoed, and the cat cried out.

She opened her eyes, seeing the animal run down the trail as Everett chased it on his horse, firing his gun in the air a few more times until the big cat vanished. He jerked the horse to a stop, watching the trail for a moment before he turned and galloped toward the tree, jumping off his horse before he could even stop it.

Lillian climbed down and ran for him, wrapping her arms around him as she reached him. He held on to her with a tight grip.

"Thank the Lord I got here in time," he said. "Are you all right?"

Her eyes filled with tears, and they streamed down her cheeks.

He pulled away from her, sliding his hands up her cheeks and holding her face. He leaned in, slumping his body down so they were eye to eye. "Are you all right?"

She nodded. "I'm sorry."

"No, you don't have to apologize. It's me who needs to. I'm so sorry that I upset you enough that you decided to run off."

"It's not your fault I did what I did. It's all mine."

He hugged her again, and although she trembled against him, she felt him shake against her.

"Oh, Lord, if I hadn't gotten here in time . . ." His voice

trailed off for a moment. "I couldn't have gone on. I just couldn't have gone on without you."

"Without me? You still . . . you still have feelings for me? After all I did? After all I told you?"

He heaved a deep sigh and grabbed her face again. His skin was warm on her cheeks. "Do you think I wouldn't want or couldn't love a widow? Because I don't care about that. It doesn't matter to me." He moved closer to her, and she could feel the warmth of his body. His grip on her face tightened, but not hard enough to hurt, just hard enough to show it was only out of love and passion, as though he was desperate for her to believe the words he said. "I swear, it doesn't matter. I would take you if you had five husbands. Ten husbands. Although I would say after ten husbands, I might be a little suspicious of whether or not you are cursed or something."

They both laughed.

"But even then . . . it would be a curse I would take and go to my deathbed a happy man."

He chuckled again, and although she wanted to, she couldn't.

"And the baby?" she asked, both wanting to know his answer and fearing it.

"Do you mean my son or daughter?" He cocked his head to the side, smiling. "He or she will not be my blood, but I don't care. I'll love and raise him or her as my own, treating them no different than I will treat our own kids if God allows."

"Are you sure that I'm . . . that we are what you want?"

"Lillian, I couldn't be surer of anything else." He leaned in, kissing her. "We should get you back to camp. Your parents are so worried, and I left without even telling them I would look for you."

"All right."

He released her as he glanced around and then reached for his horse. "Come on. Let's get you back in the saddle."

FIFTEEN

LILLIAN

*L*illian and Everett rode and walked back to the camp in silence, and although there were a few times she would try to climb down from the saddle, Everett shook his head, patting her on the leg as if to tell her to stay put. Although she wanted to get down to walk with him, she did as he asked, staying on the horse while he walked beside it.

She didn't want to think about what had happened. The fight. The storm. The mountain lion. It had been a whirlwind of events that made no sense except that it seemed to have brought them together, and she hoped that the rest of their lives would be a lot less eventful.

Now there was just one last thing to do.

She didn't know what to say to her parents when she saw them. But she knew she would have to tell them the truth about everything. It was what she owed them. It was what they deserved.

It wasn't long before they came upon the camp, and while everyone watched as Everett and Lillian approached, her parents ran for them, hugging them both after Lillian climbed down.

"Where have you been?" her mother asked, holding Lillian so tight she struggled to breathe.

"I'm sorry for worrying you, and I'm sorry for running off."

"It's all right. We forgive you."

"It would be nice if you never did it again, though." Her father hugged her and then shook Everett's hand. "Thank you for going after her."

"Of course."

"Why did you run off?" her mother asked. She cocked her head to the side and her eyebrows furrowed with concern and pain.

"It was foolish of me. I just thought it would be better. I've lied to everyone."

"I don't understand, dear."

"The reason I asked to leave home was because of Mr. Sanderson. Jacob borrowed money from him, and it was money I couldn't pay back. I didn't know what else to do, so I lied to you, telling you that I wanted to leave right away."

Her mother glanced at her father. "Should you tell her?"

"Tell me what?"

Her father laid his hand on her shoulder. "We knew about the whole thing, and I paid Mr. Sanderson the loan."

"You did? How did you find out?"

"Jacob took the money out to buy the house next to ours. We told him to wait, but he didn't want to. He wanted you to have it so bad. When I found out what he'd done, I went to Mr. Sanderson and paid the loan."

"So, we didn't have to leave? Why did you sell the house and leave with me if you knew?"

"Because we knew that deep down, loan or no loan, you needed to leave. That town was far too full of memories that only would have haunted you." Her mother looked at Everett and smiled. "Besides, you two wouldn't have met if we hadn't left."

"I can't believe you knew." Lillian dropped her gaze to the ground. She wasn't angry, not in the slightest; she just felt guilty.

"To be quite honest," her mother touched her chin, lifting it until Lillian met her gaze, "I think we needed to leave too. We don't care that we left. We are actually excited for the new start." She glanced at Everett again. "And for the son-in-law."

Everett cleared his throat, tucking his chin to his chest for a moment before a slight chuckle whispered through his chest.

"Do you disagree?" Her mother asked him.

"Oh no. I don't. I have every intention to marry your daughter."

"Good." She glanced back at Lillian. "Perhaps we should pull my old wedding dress out of the trunk then.

Lillian chuckled, shaking her head. "May I at least eat some breakfast first? I'm starving."

Everett and her parents laughed, and as her parents made their way back to the wagon, Everett held her behind.

"What do you think of the name Marie?"

"You mean if it's a girl?"

"Yes."

"I like it. But what if the baby is a boy?"

"I don't know," he said, pausing then giving her a wink. "I think I'll let you pick that one."

He kissed her again, inhaling a deep breath as he pulled away and wrapped his arms around her. "Are you happy?"

"More than I ever thought I would be again."

"Good. Let's eat some breakfast and then get hitched."

THE END

LOVE HER WAGON TRAIN COWBOY

READ BOOK FOUR IN THE WAGON TRAIN SERIES

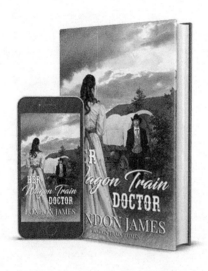

She's a nurse escaping the bleak future without the job she loves.

He never wants to be a doctor again.

ORDER HER WAGON TRAIN DOCTOR

And turn the page for a sneak peek at Book Four in the Wagon Train Women Series.

ONE

SADIE

*W*hat happens when we fail the one we love? Is it a disappointment they will hold on to forever? Or is it one they will forgive and forget?

Sadie thought it depended on the crime.

Perhaps she was right.

Perhaps she was wrong.

She'd made enough mistakes in life, and she hoped she was forgiven.

But what happens when the ones we love fail us? Was it a shoe on the other foot type of thing? The choice laid out before us just as it was for them—hold on to the hurt or let it go?

That was when she figured it would depend on the crime, and while there was a lot that Doctor Bennett Brown had done to her in her life, the last thing . . . the something that was her disappointment . . . well that she decided she would hold on to.

Forever.

. . .

*S*urgery. The ultimate thrill for a doctor. The moment when your skills are tested, and your heart is pumping. You hold a life in your hands and want nothing more than to save it.

At least that's how it was for Sadie.

"Needle, please?" Doctor Brown asked, holding out his hand. She looked over at the tray next to them and grabbed it, giving it to him. "Now, we need to stitch him up and see if it worked."

The man lying on the table under them was Mr. Matthew Dawson. Sadie had known him most of her life, and while she knew he was a troublemaker when they were younger, she hadn't been prepared to fix a gunshot wound to his shoulder.

She held the skin tight while Doctor Brown slipped the needle through it, folding the thread over and over as he stitched the wound.

"Are you sure you don't want me to do this?" she asked, hoping he would let her help as her father did.

"No, I'll do it." Doctor Brown looked down at the needle as he pulled it up into the air and squinted through his spectacles.

"Because I can stitch a wound. I've done it before."

"I know you have."

His tone grated on her annoyance. "So, if you wanted to let me finish, then you can have a seat and catch your breath . . ."

He froze mid-stitch and glanced at her over his glasses without moving his head and just moving his eyes. "I don't need to catch my breath or take a seat. What I need is for you to stop asking me questions while I'm trying to stitch this wound."

If his tone had bordered condescension before, it was ten times worse now.

"And don't think you can roll your eyes or stomp your feet like you do with your father and get your way," he continued. "Because that won't work with me."

"I wasn't going to do that." She cocked her head to the side, raising one eyebrow. "I was only trying to say that if I'm going to be a doctor and help you with your practice, then don't you think I should . . . practice?"

Doctor Brown turned his gaze back to Mr. Dawson and continued stitching the wound until it was closed. He dabbed ointment on the stitches and spun away from the man on the table, heading over to the washbasin to wash his hands.

He said nothing, and just when Sadie was going to open her mouth, he spun and leaned his rump against the table with the washbasin.

He inhaled a deep breath. "About that."

"About what?" Sadie moved over to him, washing her hands before backing away from him and folding her arms across her chest. The notion that he was about to tell her something she didn't want to hear settled in her stomach.

"I don't plan on you helping me with my practice."

"Why not?"

"Because if we are to marry and start a family . . . you will be far too busy raising the children."

"But what about until then? I mean, it's not like we will marry, and a baby will come the next day."

"Even if it took months, it's still not something I wish you to do. You could catch a sickness working with patients."

"And you could too."

"That is not the point." He lifted his hand and grabbed the bridge of his nose, inhaling and exhaling another deep breath. "You will be my wife, Sadie, and as my wife, you will have to live by rules."

"Rules? A wife has rules?"

"Perhaps rules wasn't the right word. But, yes, they are like rules. I'm the doctor. Can't you be content with being the doctor's wife?"

She knew what a doctor's wife would bring to her life. Nothing but an endless array of social gatherings and parties—

thrown by them and others in town. She'd seen her own mother live through it, and while her mother was content with her role in her father's practice, Sadie knew she wouldn't be.

She wanted more.

She wanted to be a doctor.

Sucking in a deep breath, she dropped her gaze to the floor and then looked up at him. "I'm sorry, Bennett, but no. I can't be content with just being a doctor's wife."

"I beg your pardon?"

"I don't want my mother's life. She was happy with it, but I wouldn't be."

"Yes, you will. You'll see."

"No, I know I won't, and I don't want to see. It's not what I want. I'm sorry, but I can't marry you. Not knowing that you won't allow me to follow my dreams."

"Do you know what it is you are saying? What you are throwing away?"

"I'm not throwing away anything. I'm doing both of us a service. Don't you want a wife who is content with what you offer? Why would you want a miserable woman?"

"So, I make you miserable?"

"No, that's not what I meant." She lifted her hand and rubbed her forehead. "You deserve a woman who wants the things you want. She's just not me." Sadie laid her hand on his arm, offering him a slight smile. "I'm sorry if I hurt you. It was not my intention."

She moved past him, heading toward the door.

"Where will you go?" he asked. "Your father is done in this town, and he won't be able to support you."

She glanced over her shoulder, shrugging. "Perhaps I will apply at Wesleyan College."

"You won't make it without me, you know." He snorted as though he knew his words had wounded her like the gunshot wound on Mr. Dawson. Although he had long since shown her the condescending man he could be, she always forgave him in the past.

She wouldn't today.

"At least I will have tried instead of living a miserable life with the likes of you."

Before he could say another word, she stormed out the door, slamming it behind her.

Sadie bounced along as the wagon rolled down the trail, as the memory replayed in her mind. It was another dusty, sweltering day just as the other hundreds—she'd lost count of the exact number—before. Her father, John, sat next to her, humming the same tune he had for the last several days. While she had liked it at first, the longer he hummed it, the more it annoyed her.

It was the same one he often hummed while doing surgery.

And the same one that Bennett did too.

She hadn't thought much about the man who jilted her, hadn't wanted to relive the memories like the night he changed their lives forever.

"Father, must you hum that tune today?" she asked.

"I'm humming again?" Her father looked over at her; his brow was furrowed in surprise.

"Yes, you are. Don't tell me it's become such a habit you don't even know you're doing it anymore."

"I'm sorry, Sadie. I don't mean to."

She buried her face in her hands as the guilt stung her chest. "You don't have to apologize. It's me that should say I'm sorry. I didn't mean to snap at you. It's just that tune. Bennett used to hum it. I think he learned it from you."

"Well, if that's why you don't like it, then I will stop right here, right now."

His elevated tone and jerked response humored her, and she chuckled, patting him on the back.

"It's all right if it happens again. I take it that it is a favorite tune of yours. I mean, it would have to be if it's always stuck in your head."

"I got it from a music box your mother had on the dresser in our bedroom. She would open it when she was dressing in the mornings. I never asked her what the name of the song was." His smile faded. "I wish I had because now I will never know."

"I remember that music box. It's the one packed in the trunk, isn't it?" Sadie hooked her thumb over her shoulder, pointing at their belongings in the back of the wagon.

"Yes, it is."

"I wonder if one of the ladies would know it. I might unpack it and ask them the next time we make camp."

"It would be nice to know. Although, it's not like knowing will bring her back." His shoulders hunched, and Sadie patted him on the back again.

"I miss her too."

"You would never think a doctor's wife could die before her time. I mean, it seems like something that shouldn't happen."

"You couldn't have helped her. No one could figure out what was wrong with her, and she got sicker and sicker. I know what you did; it was everything you could have done for her."

"I know. It still seems . . . I suppose pointless is the word I'm looking for."

"She wouldn't have wanted you to think that."

"I know." He inhaled a deep breath, exhaling while letting his shoulders hunch even more. "I just miss her."

The two continued bouncing down the trail, and while her father soon began to hum the tune again, it didn't bother her much this time. Instead of relating the piece of music to Bennett, she would think of her mother, remembering the kind and wonderful spirit that left this earth years too soon.

"Have you thought much about our lives in Montana?" her father asked. His voice jerked her attention.

"Do you mean about the practice?"

"Well, that and other things."

"Other things like what?"

He gave her a sideways glance and smiled. "Just things . . ."

"All right, old man, what are you getting at?" she asked, cocking her head to the side as she looked at him.

He laughed. "It's just . . . well, three of your friends are now married . . ."

"You aren't going to start that again, are you?"

"Start what?"

"All the questions. Father, you know I have dreams, and while, yes, the thought of falling in love with a good man is one of them, so is becoming a doctor, and if I'm to do one, then the other one must be put aside and right now being a doctor far outweighs being a wife and mother."

"Well, I suppose I can't argue with that. You know what you want, and you aren't willing to take anything less. It's all I've ever wanted for you."

"Well, I have to take less, considering how Bennett got me kicked out of Wesleyan." She rolled her eyes, trying to shove the thoughts of that whole mess out of her head. She hadn't expected him to be so vindictive. But he had, and he had ruined everything. "But I want to do what I can. I would love a practice of my own. I'm hoping people in Swallow Hills can give me a chance even without an education." She glanced at her father again. "Well, give us a chance."

"I'll do what I can for you, Sadie. You know I will."

She didn't know how many times he'd said those words to her in her life, but no matter how many it was, this time meant more than anything. She knew what she wanted.

Now she just needed to find it.

And take it.

TWO

CHARLES

A doctor sees death every day.

Or at least Charles had.

No matter how many bodies he'd pulled from the bed, though, it's safe to say he hadn't gotten used to it, especially when one of those bodies was his own wife.

A slight growl rumbled through Charles' chest. He hadn't wanted to do this today, hadn't wanted to relive any memories. He'd done so every day for the last two years since his wife died, and he was tired of it. It wasn't that he wanted to move on with his life, but he knew he needed to.

Mary Ellen was gone.

She was never coming back.

He had to face it.

Even if he didn't know how.

He looked around the shack of a place he called home, noticing how it seemed to age right before his eyes. Although it had never been something he'd built for them to live in for a long time, he was still surprised at how little it seemed to want to last. Mary Ellen once told him that houses know when they are loved and when love is lived inside them. Perhaps that was why the walls looked like they did—falling apart. There was no love in them anymore.

Just a sorry excuse for a doctor, he thought.

A knock rapped on the door, and before he could tell whomever it was to come in, the door popped open, and Harvey poked his head in.

"Mr. Holden?" the young man said.

"Yeah?"

"Are you here?"

"Who do you think said 'yeah'?" A flicker of annoyance whispered through his tone, and he growled under his breath.

"May I come in?"

"Sure. Sure."

As the young man opened the door and stepped inside, he smiled and ran his hands through his hair. Charles glanced at the table beside him, reaching out and grasping the glass of water he'd been sipping on this morning. He took another sip.

"What can I do for you, Harvey?" he asked.

"Well, Pa was wondering if you could come to look at Fannie Mae."

"What's wrong with her now?"

"She won't eat anything." The young man threw his hands up and shook his head.

"Did she get in the garden again?"

"Not that I know of. It's not like I can ask her, ya know. She doesn't speak English, and I don't speak goat."

"Well, did you check?"

The boy looked at him like a deer who had just spotted a hunter, and Charles rubbed his forehead, letting out a deep sigh.

"All right. All right. Let's go check the garden, then check on Fannie Mae."

This is what Charles' responsibilities had been reduced to in the small town of Soda Springs. Of course, it had never been a booming town and had always been more of a rest stop for the wagon trains, but there was a time when Charles was attending to people as patients and not the town goat who, for some reason, couldn't stay away from garlic or onions.

Two things goats are supposed to stay away from.

Charles followed Harvey out of his house and down the trail, past a few of the make-shift structures people had built over the years. Soda Springs had popped up more out of necessity than an actual desire to live around the area. The springs were a great source for any medicinal needs of the people on the wagon trains, and while Charles never cared for the taste of the soda water—too bitter for his liking—most of the men who stayed around these parts liked it, saying it tasted more like beer than anything.

Something Charles knew nothing about.

If that was what beer tasted like, though, he was glad he'd never partaken in drinking the stuff. It seemed like all beer did was get men into trouble, which wasn't anything he was ever interested in either.

Trotting up to the Millers' house, Charles checked the garden before heading toward the barn.

"Where are the onions planted again?" he asked Harvey.

"Over in that corner."

Charles meandered through the plants, picking his way through so as to not step on any vegetables growing from the ground. Seeing the Millers' garden always made him feel guilty about his own. Surely, he had one, no one could survive out here without one, but compared to the Millers', his looked about as pathetic as the definition of pathetic could get. He only grew just enough to get him by each month while preparing for the winter, and even then, there were times his dinner consisted of a huge slab of venison without potatoes or green beans on the side.

Sometimes he missed the dinners his wife used to make, while other times he enjoyed not having all the work required to have a more . . . tasteful diet as his wife always used to say they needed.

"Here they are," he said to himself, finding the long green onion stems. "And sure enough . . ." He let his voice trail off as he studied the goat prints in the dirt around the onions and the stems that looked chopped in half. Although none were dug up, upon checking the garlic next, there were three holes and half-eaten cloves lying in the dirt with more hoof prints. "It looks like she got into the garlic, mostly. Let's go have a look at her."

Charles had never once imagined that in all the years he went to school and studied to become a doctor, he would play nursemaid to a goat. And yet, here he was, doing just that, and he shook his head as he followed Harvey into the barn and into the stall where Fannie Mae was kept. The goat stood in the corner with her eyes closed as though she'd been sleeping, and she opened them as Charles walked through the gate. Her tail wagged, and she bleated as he crouched beside her, checking the clarity of her eyes and the color of her gums.

"She doesn't look too sick. Perhaps she will just have a tummy ache for a day or so. Her eyes are clear, and her gums are pink. I would say just leave her in here with food and water. Come get me if she's not eating by tomorrow evening."

"All right. I'll let Pa know."

"Where is your Pa?"

"He took the wagon to Fort Hall and should be back tomorrow. He wants to get supplies just in case wagon trains come through here."

"Ah. Yeah, that sounds like a good idea." He stood, running his hands through his hair. That was one way to make money out here or perhaps trade for things one needed. Barter and beg, but don't steal; that's what Mr. Miller had said to him once, and what's better than bartering, selling.

"Have you ever been on a wagon train, Mr. Holden?" the young lad asked.

"My wife and I came out here in a wagon. But that was years ago, and it wasn't as far away as Missouri."

"Yeah, that's like my family. Although we came out when I was a small boy, and I don't remember much. I would think that it would be a great adventure."

"Yes, I suppose it is."

"I asked Pa if I could leave with the next one that rolled in through Soda Springs, but he said no. He said I had to wait another couple of years."

"That doesn't sound so bad. I know a year seems long, but it isn't."

"But what if there aren't more wagons that come through here? The last one that came through there were men talking about people taking these things called trains. I don't want to take a train to Oregon."

The boy reminded Charles of how he was at that age. Sixteen and full of life, he wanted to start what he thought would be the adventure of a lifetime and had little patience for anything else. Charles even remembered saying Harvey's words about waiting to go to college to his father. Charles didn't want to wait either.

"If your life is meant to be lived in Oregon, then getting there shouldn't matter. Whether it's by train or wagon, and even if there are trains, I'm sure if you wanted to take a wagon, well, then that's your choice."

"I suppose you're right." Harvey looked down at the ground and kicked a rock near his shoe, watching it roll.

"I know it's hard wanting something you can't have yet. I was the same way. But if you just wait, it will come. I promise."

"Thanks, Mr. Holden."

Charles laid his hand on the boy's shoulder before giving him a few slaps on the back and making his way out of the barn. For a moment, he almost envied the boy. Not because the boy was under his parent's rule, but envied the boy's zest and hope for a life he had yet to live. Charles had been that young man once; waiting until he could go to college had been a challenging few years, but he'd done it. And then there were the years he studied. He loved every minute of them, and by the time he graduated and found Mary Ellen . . .

There wasn't anything that was going to stop them.

At least not until an infection took her from him.

Now, he felt like only a shell of the man he once was, and he hated it. Hated it but didn't know how to change it.

He glanced around the small town that had grown up around the springs. Mostly families, there were a few old men who wanted to spend the rest of their days in the quietness of Idaho, earning a little money here and there from people heading West to make a new life for themselves. He never wanted to be like those old men, yet that was what he had turned into.

Do you want to change, he thought to himself. Then you have to make the change happen.

He didn't know what that meant, but he would hope and pray that God would bring him the answer.

And soon.

"Mr. Holden!" Harvey called out.

Charles turned as the boy pointed off in the distance. Although the sun blinded him as he squinted, the bright white bonnets of several wagons caught his attention, and for the first time in he didn't know how long, his heart thumped with bubbling excitement.

"Do you know who it is?" Harvey asked, trotting up to him.

"No, I don't."

"So, does that mean . . . does that mean . . ."

"Yes, Harvey. That means it's a wagon train."

And it was just the change that Charles needed.

BRIDES OF LONE HOLLOW

Five men looking for love . . .

Five women with different ideas . . .

One small town where they all will either live happily ever after or leave with shattered dreams.

ORDER THE SERIES TODAY OR READ FOR FREE WITH KINDLE UNLIMITED

TURN THE PAGE FOR A SNEAK PEEK AT BOOK ONE, HER MAIL ORDER MIX-UP.

ONE

CULLEN

"God never gives you what He can't carry you through."

Pastor Duncan's words repeated in Cullen McCray's mind as he glanced down at his niece. All of just nine years old, the little girl sat beside him in the wagon as they drove into town. Her little body bumped into his every time a wheel rolled over a rock, and her white-blonde hair blew in the gentle breeze. She was the purest example of what the pastor was talking about. Or at least that was what the pastor had told him when he brought her to Cullen's cabin that day, scared and sad. Her entire world was torn apart by her father's sudden death and him, her uncle, her only chance.

She glanced back at him. Her eyes---his brother's eyes---stared at him. She looked more like Clint every day, and he wondered if she would grow up to have Clint's mannerisms. Would she act like him? Talk like him? Would she think like him? While he wanted her to, a part of him didn't. He wasn't sure he wanted another Clint in his life.

"What do we need from town today, Uncle Cullen?" Sadie asked.

He rolled the piece of straw from one side of his lips to the other, chewing a little more on the sweet taste of the dried stem. "Just the usual, Sadie. Did you need something else this time?"

She shrugged. "I was thinking of making a pie when we got back to the ranch."

Pie.

He hadn't thought of pie in months, hadn't thought about much of the things his late wife used to bake, actually. Because thinking of them would have reminded him of her and how she wasn't around to bake them anymore. He ate chili and stew and steak and potatoes and eggs and bacon, which was the sum of his diet. Perhaps he would have some bread or biscuits on those cold winter nights when he needed something to stick to the sides of his gut and keep him warm, but other than that, he didn't branch out. He didn't want to. He didn't want the reminder.

Of course, he knew that needed to change now that Sadie was in his life. He had to care for her, and a little growing girl needed more nourishment than what he'd been putting into his body. She needed a garden with lots of vegetables and an orchard with fruit trees. She needed bread. She needed cakes and cookies and, well, pie. All the things his late wife would spend her days making for him. He could still smell all the scents in the house. But back to the point. Sadie needed more, and she also needed to cook and bake—or at least learn to do those things along with how to sew, read, and do arithmetic.

"Do you know how to bake a pie?" he asked the girl.

"I do. Well, sort of. It was one thing Nanny Noreen taught me before . . ." The little girl's voice trailed off. She didn't want to say before the accident. She never did. She always stopped herself when she found the words trying to come out of her lips.

Not that he blamed her. He never wished to speak of it, either. His brother and his sister-in-law were now up in Heaven with his wife, leaving Sadie and him down here on earth to pick up the pieces as best as they could.

"What kind of pie did you want to make?" he asked; a slight hope rose in his chest that the girl would say peach or apple. Those were always his favorite.

"I don't know. I guess whatever fruit I can find in town."

Find in town.

Guilt prickled in his chest. She shouldn't have to find fruit in town. She should be able to go out and pick it off her tree. It was just another thing he mentally put on his list of things to do for her—plant some trees.

"Well, I suppose we can look to see what Mr. Dawson has. If you find something that works, we can get it. Did you need anything else for a pie?"

"I don't know. I suppose if I may, I'll look around?"

"Yeah. You can do that."

She glanced at him again and smiled before leaning her head on his arm.

His heart gave another little tug at his guilt. For so many months after the accident and after Pastor Duncan brought her up to his cabin, he hadn't wanted her to stay. Not quite a burden, but almost there. He had packed her bags, he didn't know how many times, fully intent on taking her down to the orphanage where he thought she belonged. She needed a chance at a family with a ma and pa. She didn't need a gruff lone wolf like him. Not to mention, he had wished to live his life alone in his cabin. The cattle ranch. The family. Those were all things Clint, his brother, wanted. He didn't. Or at least he didn't until .
. .

He shook his head, ridding himself of the thoughts of his late wife.

He couldn't think of her.

Not now.

Not today.

Never again.

He tapped the reins on the horses' backs, then whistled at them to pick up the pace into a trot. He needed the distraction of town to ease his mind.

~

MAGGIE

"*L*ove always, Clint." Maggie once again read the ending words of Clint's last letter as the stagecoach rolled down the lane. Her heart thumped, and she bit her lip as she leaned back in the seat and rested her head back.

She didn't want to think about the life she left to travel hundreds of miles across the United States so she could marry a man she didn't know. Or how she fled her parents' house in the middle of the night with her mother telling her to leave while her father slept. She only wanted to think about the life she was about to start as Mrs. Clint McCray. It didn't matter that they hadn't actually met before and had only corresponded with letters. Nor did it matter that she wasn't exactly in love with him . . . yet. It only mattered that in those letters, he promised her a life far away from her parents and the life they had planned for her. One where Daddy would shove her into a love-less marriage with either Benjamin Stone or Matthew Cooper—two sons of business acquaintances he'd known for years. She knew both men well, too. Benjamin was nothing but a bore, and Matthew . . . well, let her just say she didn't care for the way he treated women. Not to mention, his reputation in town left little to be desired, and she doubted the perpetual bachelor would even want to marry. He had more fun pursuing other tastes.

While she knew her daddy didn't think they were the best choices, he also wasn't about to have a spinster for a daughter, and she knew her time was fast ticking away. As did her mama. Which was why, when Clint's letter arrived with the plan for her to leave, they packed her a suitcase and bought her a ticket out west. Out to Lone Hollow, Montana.

"Are you headed to Lone Hollow?" the woman sitting across from her asked. Slightly older than Maggie, her hair was styled in a tight bun at the base of her neck, and she looked through a pair of spectacles resting on her long, thin nose.

"Yes, I am. My soon-to-be husband lives there and is waiting for me."

The woman smiled and ducked her chin slightly. "Best wishes to you both."

"Thank you. I'm Maggie, by the way. Maggie Colton."

The woman nodded. "Amelia Hawthorn. It's a pleasure to meet you."

"You, too." Maggie shifted her gaze from the woman to the window of the stagecoach. Nothing but mountains and forests and wilderness, Montana had been nothing like she'd ever seen before. So pretty. So peaceful. Like God's perfect place and glory was here in this state. "Where are you headed?" she asked, turning her attention to the woman.

"Brook Creek. It's about forty miles west of Lone Hollow."

"So, you still have a bit to go in your travels."

"Unfortunately. But I figure I've been this far. As long as I get to my post, I don't mind the distance."

"Post?"

"I'm a schoolteacher, and I received my post orders for the small town. I had asked for Lone Hollow, seeing as how it's a milling town, but was told it was filled . . . at least for now."

"A milling town? Does that make it a more appealing post?"

"A little. Lone Hollow has one of the few sawmills around,

and having a sawmill means more amenities than Brook Creek, like a hotel and café. There is more of a population in Lone Hollow than in Brook Creek, too, which means there are more families and children. They told me they would tell me if the teacher in Lone Hollow leaves, and if he does, then I will move again as I'm not sure I want to stay in Brook Creek."

The name made Maggie giggle. "It's funny that the town is named for two synonyms for a river."

"Don't get me started on that." The woman rolled her eyes and exhaled a deep sigh as she slid her fingers behind her ears, tucking any loose strands of her blonde bun behind her ears. The feathers on her maroon hat fluttered with her movement, and they matched her maroon dress. "Of course, all I care about are the children. I hope they are nice and are ready to learn."

"I'm sure they are, and you will do fine." Maggie bit her lip again at the thoughts in her head. She dropped her gaze to her hands, fidgeting with her fingers. "My husband-to-be has a daughter. She is nine years old. His first wife died of Scarlet Fever several years ago when she was just a baby. I feel awful that she was never able to meet her mother."

"Such a shame she lost her mama."

"Yes, it is. I just hope I can bond with her. I don't wish to replace her mother, but I hope to be someone she can accept and love."

"I'm sure she will. It might take some time, but you will do just fine."

Maggie glanced at the woman and smiled as she nodded. She didn't know if she could talk anymore about the young girl or her concerns, for the notions brought more butterflies to her stomach than the thoughts of meeting Clint. She wanted to do right by the young girl and wanted to be someone the girl could trust, look up to, and perhaps love after time had passed. She knew how wonderful it was to grow up with a mother, and she wanted that for Sadie.

The stagecoach slowed, and with the change of pace, Maggie glanced out the window again. While the mountains and forests were still in her view, a few houses speckled what little she could see, and as more and more passed by, the stagecoach slowed as it finally entered the town of Lone Hollow.

TWO

CULLEN

*C*ullen halted the horses in front of the general store, and as Sadie climbed from the wagon and trotted inside, he jumped down himself and tied the reins to the tie post. The morning sun shone down on the back of his neck, causing a thin layer of sweat that he wiped away after yanking the handkerchief from his back pocket. He made a mental note of the things he needed—sugar, flour, more seeds for their new garden, and some much-needed equipment to help him with the tasks. How Clint had tended to the old garden they had at the ranch in past years with the broken and rusted tools in the barn, he didn't know.

He also didn't want to forget he needed nails for the lumber he picked up from the sawmill the other day. The old barn had a wall that needed fixing before winter set in, or else he didn't think it would withstand another few months of the wind, ice, and snow.

Actually, the whole thing needed fixing—or to be replaced—but he wanted to at least take it one wall at a time.

"Good morning, Mr. McCray." Mr. Dawson smiled as Cullen

entered the store. His voice boomed over the bell that chimed as the door opened the closed.

"Morning."

"I saw Sadie run past a few minutes ago. She darted over in the corner as though she was determined to find something." The owner slightly chuckled as he adjusted his glasses up his nose.

"She's fixing to make a pie this afternoon."

"Oh? A pie. Sounds delicious. I have some nice apples that Mr. Smith brought in yesterday from his orchard. I tried one myself, and they are bright red on the outside and juicy on the inside. They should make some lovely pies."

"Well, then I suppose I see an apple pie in my future for dinner, then."

The two men chuckled at Cullen's joke as Cullen leaned against the counter.

"So, what can I do for you today?" Mr. Dawson asked.

"Just the usual. Plus, I need a new rake, hoe, and shovel. I'm going to expand the garden at the ranch this spring. Let Sadie have fun growing what we will eat in the winter."

"Sounds like she'll enjoy that."

Cullen ducked his chin for a moment, lowering his voice. "I sure hope so."

Mr. Dawson laid his hand on Cullen's shoulder. "Mrs. Dawson and I were talking about what happened to your brother and how you've taken the girl in and cared for her. You're doing a mighty fine thing, Mr. McCray, and a mighty fine job, too. The whole town thinks so. You shouldn't doubt yourself."

Cullen nodded. "Thank you. I'm trying. Sometimes I do not know why God gave a guy like me a girl to raise."

"Because He knows what He's doing."

The door opened, and the bell above it chimed again. Cullen glanced over, meeting Pastor Duncan's gaze as he strolled in.

The pastor nodded and tipped his hat to the two men before taking it off and tossing it on the counter.

"Morning, gentlemen," he said.

"Morning, Pastor." While Mr. Dawson returned the salutation, Cullen only nodded. An air of being uncomfortable squared in his chest. He hadn't seen the pastor in a while, and the last time he did was when the pastor brought Sadie up to his cabin with the news . . . and well, he hadn't been pleasant to the old man. In fact, he'd been downright rude, and while at the time he thought he was justified, there were times he felt he'd overreacted.

Pastor Duncan nodded back to the store owner and yanked a slip of paper from his pocket. "Mr. Dawson, I have some special requests I need to make this morning, and I'm hoping you don't have to order any of them."

"Sure thing." Mr. Dawson held out his hand. "Give me the order. I'll see what I can do after I get Mr. McCray loaded."

"Oh, there's no need for that. Just bring what you have for me out here. I'll load it myself," Cullen said, hoping the gesture would make up—even if it were just a little—for the past.

"Are you sure?"

"Yes, I'm sure. See to the Pastor's order. I'm in no hurry."

As Mr. Dawson vanished in the store's backroom, Pastor Duncan leaned against the counter. He glanced at Cullen a few times before clearing his throat. "Did you bring Miss Sadie with you?"

"She's over there, gathering things to make a pie this afternoon."

"A pie?" The pastor's eyebrows raised as he smiled. "Sounds like you will have a splendid dinner this evening."

"If she doesn't burn the house down." Cullen chuckled to himself a bit.

"It also sounds like she's doing all right. After . . . everything."

"She seems to be. She has her moments as I would expect anyone to have, having been through what she's been through."

"And how are you handling everything?"

"All right, too, I suppose." He paused for a moment, clearing his throat. "Listen, Pastor, about the last time we spoke—"

"There's nothing to say about that."

"But there is. I wasn't . . . I was rude to you, and I shouldn't have been. I can't imagine it was easy for you, bringing Sadie to my cabin with the news."

"It wasn't that bad. I figure since it was His plan, I might as well help Him orchestrate it." The pastor smiled. "We haven't seen you around church lately. I was hoping you would start coming again now that you have Sadie."

A flicker of guilt prickled in Cullen's chest. He knew how wrong it was to skip church every week. But it had been the one thing he and his wife shared, had been their favorite time together, and since her death, he hadn't been able to even think about setting foot inside that place. Every inch screamed her. Every wooden pew. Every window. The door. The pulpit. Even the floor that she'd walked down dressed in a white dress to become his wife.

Now she lay in the ground in the small graveyard next to it.

That was another reason he hadn't been back. He hadn't visited her grave since the funeral.

"I'll think about next Sunday, and I'll ask Sadie if she wants to go," he lied.

Pastor Duncan's eyes narrowed for a moment before they softened. "Children rarely know what's best for them, and it's up to their parents to tell them what they need to learn and do."

"Yeah, well, I'm not her parent."

"You are. It's just a different kind of parent."

Cullen opened his mouth to argue again but stopped himself as the little girl bounded around one of the shelves. A broad grin etched across her face as she held an armful of bright red apples.

"Uncle Cullen! Uncle Cullen! Mr. Dawson has apples. Lots of red and juicy-looking apples. I think I'll try to make an apple pie, maybe even two pies. What do you think?"

"I think it sounds delicious, Sadie."

Her smile widened even more, and she handed him every one, she carried.

"Hello, Pastor Duncan," she said, noticing him standing there.

"Good morning, Sadie. How are you this fine morning?"

"Good." A memory seemed to flicker in her mind, and her face twisted a little. Her smile faded. While Cullen wasn't sure of the thoughts suddenly weighing on her mind, he could guess that it had to do with the fact that the last time she'd seen the pastor was when he brought her to Cullen's cabin to let Cullen know, not only of his brother's death but that Sadie was now in his custody. He didn't want to imagine what that time had been like for her. Having lived through both her parents' deaths, she was now an orphan and coming to live with a man she only knew a little.

As Cullen put the apples on the counter, Mr. Dawson returned from the back with his arms full. "I was able to gather most of what you needed, Pastor Duncan," he said, setting it all down.

"It's a sign from God, then. It's going to be a great day."

Cullen stepped away from the counter as the pastor and store owner finished their transaction. A small part of him hoped the subject of church wouldn't come up again, at least not in front of Sadie, before he had a chance to talk to her. He didn't know if he wanted even to mention it, at least not until he was ready—which he was far from it—and he didn't need the pressure of being roped into it before then.

The pastor said nothing, however, and after paying for his

supplies, he tipped his hat to them, gave Sadie an extra wave and a smile, and left the store without another word.

Cullen breathed a sigh of relief as he laid his hand on Sadie's shoulder and guided her around the counter. "Let's help Mr. Dawson get our supplies from the back and then get them loaded into our wagon."

~

MAGGIE

*T*he stagecoach came to a complete stop in front of the Lone Hollow Hotel, and Maggie climbed out. Her boots touched down on the dirt road, and she lifted her hand to shield her eyes from the sun. It helped a little, but she still had to squint as she glanced from one direction to the other. Clint had said he would wait for her at the hotel, but no one had even approached her as the driver handed over her luggage. Shrugging off the slight air of confusion, she crossed the hotel's porch and sat down on a bench just outside the door. The wood planks showed little kindness to her shoes as the humid moisture in the air stuck to her skin. The sun's heat deepened, weighing on her with a heavy thickness.

Perhaps he got tied up or something and is just running late, she thought.

As the stagecoach's driver finished unloading a few parcels that were obviously en route to people who lived in the town, he climbed back into his seat and cued the horses down the road. Maggie could see Amelia wave just before the carriage vanished around the corner, and she couldn't help but smile when she thought of the small town of Brook Creek.

Who names these towns, anyway, she thought.

People meandered through the streets while Maggie continued to wait on the bench under the overhang, and she glanced around at the hotel to keep her mind busy. It wasn't the worst one she'd ever seen, but it wasn't the best either, looking as though years of weathered seasons had taken a toll on the old wood—the once bright shade of dark red paint had faded into a pale cherry color.

"Top of the mornin' to yeh, Miss," called a voice from the building across the street. She jerked her head around to find a short, plump man tipping his hat to a woman walking toward him. The woman smiled and waved as she passed, and he watched her for a moment before returning to the sweeping he had been doing on the porch in front of a building that looked like a café. The volume of his thick Irish accent over-whelmed the chirping birds in the oak trees above, and he turned his body slightly as a pair of young boys ran past him, one betting the other he could leap up and batter the painted sign while the other could not. However, upon catching the man's glare, they both seemed to realize their theory would go unproven.

More people meandered along the storefront while a man tossed supplies into the back of a wagon while a little girl watched. Her white-blonde curls bounced from not only her movement but the gentle breeze in the air.

Maggie checked her pocket watch. The stagecoach hadn't been early or late, but right on time, and a flicker of concern rested in her stomach. She had gotten the correct date, hadn't she? She reached into her handbag and yanked out the letter, unfolding it as she read it one more time.

"You should arrive on the 10th of April by wagon. I will wait for you." She read the words of Clint's letter in a whisper to herself.

Today was the 10th of April, was it not? She was certain it was.

"Good morning, Miss," a voice said.

She glanced up. Her heart thumped.

"Are you new in town?" The older gentleman said. He tipped his hat before taking it off. "My name is Pastor John Duncan."

She let out a deep breath and stood. "Miss Maggie Colton."

"Sorry for the intrusion. I just saw you sitting here, and it looked as though you were waiting for someone."

"I am. Mr. Clint McCray. I'm his . . . wife-to-be, I suppose you could say. We've been corresponding for several months, and he sent for me so we can be married." She showed him the envelope and piece of paper she was reading as though she thought it would prove her story. Not that she thought the pastor didn't believe her, it just seemed like the thing to do.

He didn't take it, and instead, he jerked his head and blinked as though shocked.

Her stomach twisted. What had she said that seemed wrong? Perhaps she should give a little more detail, hoping to gain some insight into what the pastor was thinking. "He said he would wait for me when I arrived. See? It's all here in this letter. Do you know him?"

"Well, yes, I do . . . but . . ." The pastor glanced over his shoulder, hooking his thumb. He paused for a moment as though watching someone, then turned back to her. "Actually, Mr. McCray is just over there, loading supplies into his wagon."

She had noticed the man earlier. Perhaps he had wanted to get everything loaded before he came for her. "Ah, yes, that man with his daughter. I see. Her name is Sadie, correct?"

"That would be them—Mr. McCray and Sadie McCray." Pastor Duncan moved, stepping aside and motioning her toward the road as if to give her permission to cross it so she could finally be with the one she'd been waiting on. "It was a pleasure meeting you, Miss Colton."

"The pleasure is all mine." She shook his hand again, then bent down, grabbing her suitcases before she looked in both directions and trekked across the road.

Her heart thumped with each step, and as she neared Clint,

she blew out a breath. This was it. This was their moment. The one she could picture in her mind. He would smile. She would smile. They would hug and tell each other how happy they were to meet each other finally. He was more handsome than she had even thought. With broad shoulders and this rough exterior with chocolate hair, a subtle beard, and arms that as they tossed bags of supplies in the wagon, she imagined them wrapped around her. Her excitement fluttered in her chest, and she had to remind herself to walk, not run, to him.

"Mr. McCray?" she called out, and as Clint turned to face her, she dropped her bags and threw her arms out, wrapping them around his neck. Perhaps it wasn't exactly proper of her, but she couldn't help herself, not to mention she didn't care. "I can't believe we are finally meeting."

Clint wiggled from her grasp and backed away from her. His eyes grew wide, and his mouth gaped for a moment. "Who are you?" he asked.

"What do you mean, who am I? I'm Maggie, Maggie Colton. Your soon-to-be wife. You sent for me, and you were supposed to meet me. Remember? It's the 10th of April." Her stomach twisted with each of her words, and with each passing second that the words didn't seem to bring any clarity to him. She still had his letter in her hand, and she outstretched it. "You wrote me, telling me to come so that you and I would be married."

ORDER THE SERIES TODAY OR READ FOR **FREE** WITH KINDLE UNLIMITED

To my sister
Michelle Renee Horning

April 3, 1971 - January 8, 2022
*You will be forever missed. I don't know how I'm going to do this thing
called life without you.*

LONDON JAMES IS A PEN NAME FOR ANGELA CHRISTINA ARCHER. SHE LIVES ON A RANCH WITH HER HUSBAND, TWO DAUGHTERS, AND MANY FARM ANIMALS. SHE WAS BORN AND RAISED IN NEVADA AND GREW UP RIDING AND SHOWING HORSES. WHILE SHE DOESN'T SHOW ANYMORE, SHE STILL LOVES TO TRAIL RIDE.

FROM A YOUNG AGE, SHE ALWAYS WANTED TO WRITE A NOVEL. HOWEVER, EVERY TIME THE DESIRE FLICKERED, SHE SHOVED THE THOUGHT FROM MY MIND UNTIL ONE MORNING IN 2009, SHE AWOKE WITH THE DETERMINATION TO FOLLOW HER DREAM.

WWW.AUTHORLONDONJAMES.COM

JOIN MY MAILING LIST FOR NEWS ON RELEASES, DISCOUNTED SALES, AND EXCLUSIVE MEMBER-ONLY BENEFITS!

Made in the USA
Monee, IL
23 January 2024

52253558R00090